Enjoy all of these American Girl Mysteries®:

THE SILENT STRANGER   A *Kaya* Mystery

LADY MARGARET'S GHOST   A *Felicity* Mystery

SECRETS IN THE HILLS   A *Josefina* Mystery

THE RUNAWAY FRIEND   A *Kirsten* Mystery

SHADOWS ON SOCIETY HILL   An *Addy* Mystery

CLUE IN THE CASTLE TOWER   A *Samantha* Mystery

SECRETS AT CAMP NOKOMIS   A *Rebecca* Mystery

MISSING GRACE   A *Kit* Mystery

CLUES IN THE SHADOWS   A *Molly* Mystery

THE SILVER GUITAR   A *Julie* Mystery

and many more!

— A *Rebecca* MYSTERY —

A BUNDLE
OF TROUBLE

by Kathryn Reiss

★ American Girl®

Questions or comments? Call 1-800-845-0005, visit our
Web site at **americangirl.com**, or write to Customer Service,
American Girl, 8400 Fairway Place, Middleton, WI 53562-0497.

Printed in China
11 12 13 14 15 16 LEO 10 9 8 7 6 5 4 3 2 1

PICTURE CREDITS
The following individuals and organizations have generously
given permission to reprint illustrations contained in "Looking Back":
pp. 164–165—Library of Congress, Prints & Photographs Division, Detroit
Publishing Company Collection, [LC-D4-10865] (Mulberry Street); *Little Italy,
1898*, Museum of the City of New York, The Byron Co. Collection (family on
stoop); pp. 166–167—Library of Congress, Prints & Photographs Division, Bain
Collection, [LC-USZ62-71330] (children playing on sidewalk with carriage);
Library of Congress, Prints & Photographs Division, Jacob Riis Collection,
[LC-USZ62-22845] (girl with baby sister); Brown Brothers (newsboy); Library of
Congress, Prints & Photographs Division, Bain Collection, [LC-UDZ62-119372]
(boys playing leapfrog); pp. 168–169—The Photographic Collections, University
of Maryland, Baltimore County (boys gambling); From The New York Times,
© September 10, 1909. All rights reserved. Used by permission and protected
by the Copyright Laws of the United States (kidnapping news clipping);
Newseum collection (newspaper front page); Associated Press (wanted poster);
pp. 170–171—Library and Archives Division, Historical Society of Western
Pennsylvania, Pittsburgh, PA (girls with corno charms); Photo courtesy of the
Rosi-Kessel family (family sukkah).

Illustrations by Sergio Giovine

Cataloging-in-Publication Data
available from the Library of Congress

To my "Play Group Tea Ladies"—Sangeeta, Katie, Sheri, Leslie, and Kathy—whose weekly chats about our own bundles of trouble have provided more than a decade of laughter, encouragement, and comfort: this one's for you.

And a special welcome to a brand new bundle: Hannah June Elliott Kaganovich, born June 9, 2010

Huge thanks, too, to Laura Klaus Abada for stories of Sukkot celebrations, and to Louise Reiss for her Italian expertise. Grazie!

TABLE OF CONTENTS

1

A Noise in the Night

Rebecca stood on the castle balcony, still and alert. She cupped her hand to her ear, listening for a cry in the fading light. Suddenly she stiffened, looked up, and gasped. The baby! Her face hardened into a mask of determination. In an instant she lifted the skirts of her velvet gown in one hand, turned, and started climbing the stone wall behind her. At the top, she inched along the ledge until she reached the niche where the villain had left the baby in peril. Sweeping the swaddled bundle up into her arms, she clutched it to her chest, closed her eyes, and heaved a great sigh of relief—

"And . . . cut!" yelled the director. "Perfect, Miss Rubin!"

As Rebecca turned to smile at the director,

her golden crown toppled from her head, spinning down and down, landing with a loud THUMP!—and Rebecca woke up.

She sat up in bed, eyes wide. *Only a dream!* But such an exciting dream until... what had awakened her?

Moonlight streamed through the window. Rebecca could see the twin lumps of her older sisters in the bed across the room. The parlor clock chimed twice. She cuddled back under her quilts and lay listening to the silence.

One of her sisters stirred.

Then Rebecca heard footsteps.

Someone else was awake at two o'clock in the morning. She slipped out of bed. The floorboards were cold against her bare feet. From the parlor she heard the creak of the couch as her brother Victor turned over. Through the closed door of her parents' bedroom she heard the familiar sound of Papa's snores. She tiptoed through the kitchen and peeked into the parlor, where her brothers slept. There they were: seven-year-old Benny snuggled up across two chairs pushed together for his bed, and fourteen-year-old Victor stretched out on the couch.

Rebecca waited, frowning. Something didn't seem right. She scanned the shadowed room, but all seemed as usual. The clock on the mantel ticked. Mama's sewing lay folded on the armchair. Benny's shoes were placed neatly under the window.

Victor let out a little snore, like Papa. Reassured, Rebecca headed back to bed.

But when she tried to recapture her movie dream, sleep wouldn't come. Instead she kept seeing Benny's little shoes, standing properly under the window.

Something was strange about those shoes, and as she drifted toward sleep she realized what it was: Only Benny's shoes were there. Victor's shoes were on his feet; one of them had been sticking out from the blanket on the couch.

What was her brother up to?

⚜

A Bundle of Trouble

The next thing Rebecca knew, it was Sunday morning and her sisters were standing over her. A weak autumn sun streamed through the bedroom window. "Wake up, Beckie!" said sixteen-year-old Sophie. "Breakfast is ready."

"Mama says please tell Victor to hurry up," added Sadie as the twins left the room, their identical skirts swishing.

Rebecca groaned, sitting up sleepily. As she put on her dressing gown and followed the good smells coming from the kitchen, she stopped at her parents' bedroom door. Victor was leaning over their washstand.

"Breakfast is ready—" she began, then broke off, staring at his nightshirt. Streaks of dirt soiled the white cotton. "Gosh! What happened to *you?*"

Her brother looked around, startled. He flushed. "Oh—nothing." He grabbed his dressing gown from the peg on the wall and hurriedly pulled it over the nightshirt. "Maybe I was dreaming about exploring a cave—you know, like Tom Sawyer."

Rebecca remembered the shoes on his feet in bed. *A dream doesn't leave dirt stains*, she thought wryly. She knew that Mama and Papa were already concerned because Victor had not been doing his homework lately, preferring to go out with pals after school. He had come home late for dinner several times. Yesterday he had been sent on an errand for Mama but did not return until the family was halfway through their evening meal. Papa had been angry, and Victor was forbidden to leave the apartment after supper. Now Victor looked as if he'd hardly slept.

Had he gone out to meet his friends against Papa's orders—and the noise of his return had awakened her? Had Victor leaped under the covers, shoes still on his feet, when she came into the parlor?

"I'll be there in a minute," Victor mumbled. "Now, scram!"

Rebecca rolled her eyes, and went to the kitchen. Mama was toasting thick slices of bread at the black cast-iron stove. Bubbie and Grandpa,

Rebecca's grandparents who lived upstairs in the same apartment building, had come down for breakfast. "Good morning," Rebecca greeted her family.

Before she could decide whether to mention Victor's nightshirt, Papa looked up from his newspaper. "Some good news," he said.

"What is it, Papa?" asked Sophie as Sadie peered over his shoulder. Victor slipped into the kitchen, yawning.

Papa read the headline aloud: "Kidnapped Baby Safe."

"Oh—such a relief!" cried Mama.

"I haven't stopped thinking about that little boy," said Sadie.

"Me neither," Rebecca agreed. Maybe she had even rescued the baby in her movie dream because she'd been worrying so much about the real-life baby who had been kidnapped three days before.

"Read us the details, Papa!" urged Sophie. They all listened as they ate Mama's warm bread.

Kidnapped Baby Safe

Late last night, six-month-old Christopher Porter was discovered in a basket on the steps of St. Michael's Church, several miles from where he was stolen last Thursday. According to police, the baby was found unharmed and attired in different clothes from those he was wearing when he was taken.

The infant had been sleeping in his buggy outside Nurden's Butcher Shop in Manhattan while his young mother shopped, when someone snatched him, leaving behind a ransom note demanding $100. The whole city feared for the baby's safety. The young parents did not have such funds readily available, but donations poured in from generous neighbors and friends, and those sums, added to the couple's scant savings, were placed, as the note demanded, in a bag under a bush in Central Park last evening. The ransom note cautioned that no police and no family members were to be present when the money was collected, or the parents would never see their son again.

Mr. and Mrs. Porter extend their most heartfelt gratitude for the help of their friends and for the safe return of their son.

"Would you pay so much money to get *me* back?" interrupted Benny, wide-eyed.

Mama ruffled his hair. "I would do anything to keep you safe."

"You think is only here people disappear?" Grandpa asked solemnly. "In our village in Russia, overnight people disappear—and they never come back."

Bubbie shuddered. "The tsar and his soldiers," she said. "Always stirring up trouble for the Jews."

"This is why we leave Russia and come to America," said Grandpa, placing his hand over Bubbie's.

Now, as if talk of kidnapped babies had triggered it, the wail of an unhappy baby filled the air. Rebecca could hear voices coming up the stairwell outside their apartment door. There were thuds and a scraping sound, followed by more voices.

"That must be the new neighbors moving in downstairs," Mama said. "I heard they were coming soon."

"Oh, let's go meet them!" Rebecca said eagerly.

Papa turned to Victor. "You will stay here. We need to have a talk."

Uh-oh, Rebecca thought. Did Papa know that Victor had sneaked out?

2
NEW NEIGHBORS

"You go meet new neighbors," Bubbie said. "Me, I am rushing back upstairs. Bread is baking in my oven!" She and Grandpa headed for the door. "When is ready, we take fresh loaf to the new family."

Rebecca hurriedly tied on an apron and went to the sink to help her sisters wash the breakfast dishes. Mama smoothed her long skirts, tidied her thick dark hair, and then wrapped jars of homemade pickled onions and jam in brown paper. After Rebecca dried the last bowl, they all went downstairs to welcome the new neighbors. The cries of the baby they had heard earlier grew louder.

"Will there be someone for me to play with?" asked Benny hopefully.

"Well, someone is certainly making a racket," teased Sadie. "He could be your age."

A well-used wicker baby buggy stood in the hall outside one of the two small ground-floor apartments. The door had been left ajar, and it swung open as Mama knocked, revealing a parlor considerably smaller than the Rubins', with only one window. A morning breeze wafted into the room, where half a dozen people were opening boxes, arranging furniture, and sweeping the corners with a broom. *Oh my goodness*, Rebecca thought. How could such a large family live here comfortably?

A man with a drooping mustache came over to greet Rebecca's family. He was as tall as Papa but younger, rail thin, and rather pale—what Mama called "peaked." Still, his smile was warm as he accepted Mama's gifts and introduced himself as Morris Brodsky. He told them he and his wife, Naomi, would be living here with their four-month-old baby, Nora. The tall woman holding the baby was his cousin, Miriam. The other people were more cousins and friends, helping with the move.

Rebecca, standing in the doorway, was relieved that not all these people would be living in this small apartment after all. But oh, how she wished someone would quiet that poor baby! Little dark-haired Nora writhed in the arms of Cousin Miriam, who murmured soothing words, trying to calm her. The baby's squalls filled the room, and Benny clapped his hands over his ears. Rebecca wanted to put her hands over her own ears but worried it might be rude.

As if on an island apart from the hustle and bustle, a young woman sat in a rocking chair by the open window. She was small and thin, with a cloud of curly dark hair piled up in a haphazard bun. Her head was bowed.

Mr. Brodsky spoke to her. "My dear, we have our first visitors. This is Mrs. Rubin and her children—young Benjamin, then Rebecca, and twins Sadie and Sophie." His smile was wry. "I'm sure in time I'll know which twin is which!"

The woman raised her head and smiled

at them. She got to her feet. "Pleased to make your acquaintance," she said in a soft voice as Mr. Brodsky took her hand and led her over to Mama. "I'm afraid I'm not able to tell which of you are twins and which aren't, but I hope to soon know you by your voices."

Rebecca saw that Mrs. Brodsky's eyes were clouded. The skin around them was red and swollen. She had heard of something called trachoma, an eye infection that people seemed to get when they lived too crowded together. Over in the East Side tenements, where her cousin Ana used to live, many people suffered from trachoma. Some went blind.

"Morris is very worried about my eyesight," Mrs. Brodsky told them in her soft voice. Rebecca had to lean close to hear her over the howling baby. "But I am worrying about *him*—working two jobs so that we can afford this new apartment and pay the doctor for my treatment. He's always so tired after a day in the factory, and now he is also helping to tutor English at the settlement house in the evening."

"It's worth it," Mr. Brodsky said. "That tenement room was so ... well, *squalid* is the only word for it. I think that's where you caught this infection in the first place. You'll be healthier living here. We can open the window to air the room. And with running water at the sink, it will be easier to keep clean."

"But it's going to be hard for you, working so much." Mrs. Brodsky had to raise her voice to be heard over the baby. "I'm afraid we won't see much of you."

"You won't see me at all if you go blind," her husband replied grimly, pulling on his coat. "At least this way you have a chance to recover." He turned to his cousin Miriam, who was holding Nora to her shoulder, patting the small back in an attempt to quiet her. "Goodness, such a racket!" he clucked distractedly.

"And when I do recover, I'll take in sewing again," Mrs. Brodsky vowed. "That will help pay our rent, too." She turned to the Rubins. "I used to be a dressmaker," she explained.

"And a fine one," Mr. Brodsky said warmly.

Then he sighed and nodded to the Rubins. "Now, please excuse me, but I need to leave for work. I have a new tutoring appointment."

Two more men came through the door as Mr. Brodsky went out. They were carrying a table. Another entered behind them, lugging a chair. The woman holding Nora turned to Mama. "I've been helping Naomi and Morris out as best I can this morning," she said. "Would you mind holding Nora while I prepare a tonic for Naomi's eyes?"

"Not at all," said Mama as she took the baby. Little Nora squirmed in her blankets. "My children can help carry in the boxes."

The twins and Benny hurried to bring in straight-backed chairs, a coat stand, and a box of dishes. The baby in Mama's arms fretted. Rebecca stroked her soft hair.

"I don't know why she's so unhappy this morning," Mrs. Brodsky said apologetically. "She's usually such a quiet baby." She shut her eyes for a moment, then opened them to peer at her daughter. "Oh, dear. Do her eyes look all right? I'm so worried she'll catch my affliction. It's very contagious, I'm afraid."

Rebecca's eyes suddenly felt itchy. She took a step away from the baby.

"Little Nora's eyes look fine," Mama said.

"As long as we all wash our hands often with carbolic soap, no one else will contract the disease," Cousin Miriam added reassuringly. "Nora is just upset by the move. Now, you lie down, Naomi dear, and let me dose your eyes."

Rebecca watched Cousin Miriam drip a solution from a bottle into Mrs. Brodsky's eyes. Some of the solution dribbled onto the woman's cheeks, and Cousin Miriam tenderly wiped it away with cotton.

While Nora continued to wail, Rebecca longed to comfort her, but she didn't know how. The whole building could probably hear the unhappy baby. Rebecca was glad when Mama offered to help.

"If you'd like," Mama said, "we can take Nora upstairs to our apartment for a while. That way you can rest, Mrs. Brodsky."

"Why, how kind!" Cousin Miriam said, looking relieved.

"Yes, thank you so much," Mrs. Brodsky said gratefully. "Just till lunchtime, perhaps? She'll need to be fed then."

"Here, Naomi, take my arm," Cousin Miriam said. "Would you like to sit by the window again? Let me help you get settled." She smiled at Mama. "Thank you kindly, Mrs. Rubin."

"It's our pleasure," Mama said. "Beckie, can you get the door?"

Rebecca opened the apartment door and found a young woman standing in the hall just outside the door. The woman jumped back, startled. "Oh, hello!" Her thick auburn hair was worn in a fashionable pompadour and topped by a feathered hat. Her large eyes were pale blue.

"Hello," Rebecca replied. This woman did not live in their building, and Rebecca had never seen her before. "Are you looking for the Brodskys?"

"Well, yes!" The woman peered intently at Rebecca. "I believe I am. Indeed!" Her voice was warm and friendly. "Are you one of the Brodsky children?"

"No, I live upstairs," said Rebecca. "The Brodskys are just moving in."

"Oh, yes," said the woman. "I saw their cart out front."

Mama, Benny, and the girls stepped out of the Brodskys' apartment. The woman looked with interest at the fretful baby in Mama's arms. "What a good pair of lungs on your little one!"

"She's not our little one, thank goodness," said Sadie.

Mama was quick to explain. "We're just looking after Nora while our neighbors unpack, Mrs.—?"

"Oh," the woman said, appearing flustered. "Henks. I'm Mrs. Henks."

"This baby doesn't like moving," announced Benny, raising his voice over the crying.

"Well, I have little ones myself at home," Mrs. Henks said. "I know how they are. If I can ever be of help..."

"Two offers of help!" Cousin Miriam spoke

from the doorway. "You're very kind."

"I don't mind in the least," said Mrs. Henks. "We must all help our neighbors as we can." She turned away and headed back down the front steps. "Good-bye for now," she called over her shoulder. "Lovely to meet you."

"Such wonderful neighbors," murmured Mrs. Brodsky, coming to stand behind her cousin. "I think we shall be very happy here."

As Mama started upstairs with the baby, Cousin Miriam called Rebecca back. "Don't forget her rattle. It might soothe her if she's teething." She handed Rebecca a small tin rattle tied with a frayed pink ribbon. "And here is her bonnet and an extra blanket, should you take her for a walk."

Carrying these things, Rebecca followed Mama, the twins, and Benny up to their apartment. As soon as Rebecca closed the door, Mama turned to look at her girls with a smile. "So, who wants to play with a real live doll today?" The baby in her arms screwed up her face and howled.

"I have math homework!" cried Sadie.

"Geography, too!" added Sophie. "A mountain of it."

"Such dedication to their studies my children have," said Mama wryly.

Sadie eyed the red-faced baby dubiously. "Besides, I don't want to catch that eye disease."

"The baby seems healthy enough, and Mrs. Brodsky is receiving medical treatment," Mama said comfortingly. "In the meantime, we can help out."

"But I don't know a thing about babies," objected Sadie, "and I need to go to Lucy's to study for our test tomorrow."

"Me too," Sophie said quickly. "Beckie, you can look after the baby."

"I don't know how to look after a baby either," Rebecca said nervously. Then, as the baby's wailing intensified, she gazed innocently at her sisters. "Besides, I'm not old enough." Her sisters were always saying she was too young to do this or that. For once, she was happy to agree.

Mama carried the baby into the parlor. "I'll

need help from at least one of you," she said. "You're all old enough. It would be a kindness to a neighbor, Beckie," she added gently. "A *mitzvah*."

"Well," Rebecca said slowly, eyeing the baby. "I'll do it—but Sadie and Sophie have to do my chores today."

"Agreed!" shouted her sisters in relief, and they shook Rebecca's hand to seal the deal.

3

WHO IS THAT BOY?

Mama laid the baby on the couch. She showed Rebecca how to change her diaper. Nora was soaking wet and had a terrible rash. "Dear little one," crooned Mama. "No wonder you're yelling. I would yell, too."

"Maybe Mrs. Brodsky's poor eyesight keeps her from noticing the rash," said Rebecca, and Mrs. Rubin nodded.

"And of course the baby's father is seldom home—working two jobs to make ends meet," Mama added. "There's nobody to notice such things."

Unwrapped from her blankets, baby Nora kicked and fussed. Her little arms thrashed up and down, and one hand grazed Rebecca's cheek. "Ow!" exclaimed Rebecca.

"Goodness," said Mrs. Rubin. "Let's trim those nails before she scratches her own little face. Please hand me the nail scissors, Beckie."

Rebecca took the little scissors out of the drawer and helped hold the baby while Mama trimmed the nails on her fingers and toes.

"It must be hard for Mrs. Brodsky to take care of this little one with her sight failing," Mama said. "We must be good neighbors and help out as much as we can." She went to the kitchen for some cornstarch to sprinkle on the baby's rash, and then she suggested that Rebecca go to the corner drugstore for some ointment. "Take Nora along. She might enjoy the fresh air." Mama gave Rebecca a little money for the salve.

Rebecca carefully wrapped Nora in her faded pink blankets and carried her downstairs with Mama following. She settled Nora into the wicker buggy, and wheeled the buggy out to the front stoop. Mama helped lift it down to the sidewalk, and then Rebecca set off for the pharmacy.

For the first time that morning, Nora was

quiet. The movement of the wheels jostling over the cracks in the sidewalk seemed to soothe her. Outside the shop, Rebecca hesitated. She remembered the article Papa had read about the kidnapping. Although that baby was now safely home, the kidnapper had not been caught. She decided to take the buggy inside.

A lanky, dark-eyed boy about Victor's age approached the shop and gallantly held the door open so that Rebecca could maneuver the buggy over the threshold. Then he followed her in and stood looking at the jars of candies while Rebecca walked to the counter.

Morton's Pharmacy was a busy place. Its shelves were stocked with jars of pills in many colors, bottles of cough remedies and medicinal syrups, soaps and tooth powders, perfumes and ointments. Glass cases held candles and a selection of bath salts, tonics, and creams. Jars displayed mint lozenges, boiled sweets, and licorice. At the soda fountain along one wall, customers ordered hot and cold drinks and slices of seasonal fruit pie.

WHO IS THAT BOY?

Mr. Morton, the pharmacist, was stationed on a stool behind the counter at the shiny cash register. He was a slow-moving man who liked to chat with everyone. Rebecca waited now while he measured out a bottle of cod liver oil for a woman with two small children hanging on her skirts. He handed each child a licorice whip and then smiled at Rebecca.

"Now, how can I help you, young lady?"

She explained about the diaper rash, and he clucked his tongue sympathetically. "I've got just the thing," he said, selecting a small jar of white cream from the shelf. "This will fix the little one in no time."

Rebecca thanked him and handed him the money. While she waited for her change, Nora began crying again. Rebecca turned to her and found the tall, dark-eyed boy leaning over the baby, making faces.

He straightened. "She is nice baby, no?" he asked. He had a mop of black hair, a brusque voice, and a foreign accent. Rebecca wasn't sure what sort of accent it was; there were people from so many countries living in her neighbor-hood—Jews from Russia, like her own family, and Irish, Italians, Germans...

"She is prettiest baby, I think," he said, leaning over the buggy again.

Rebecca didn't really think so, because crying, red-faced babies weren't much to look at, but she nodded.

The baby quieted again as the boy grinned down at her. "You go for a walk?" he asked. "Maybe in the park? Babies, they like walk in the park."

"Maybe," Rebecca replied. She wished the boy would not stand so close to Nora.

"Is getting cold." He reached into the buggy and pulled the pink blankets up to Nora's chin. "And maybe she is hungry."

"She's fine," said Rebecca coolly, tightening her hold on the buggy handle. He didn't look old enough to be a kidnapper, but who could tell? It was unusual, surely, for a boy his age to be interested in a baby. Victor never looked twice at babies.

The boy gave her a piercing look, then turned and loped down the street.

Rebecca was relieved to see him go, and then with a start realized she had left her change on the counter inside. With a quick glance to check that the boy was not coming back, she dashed into the shop. As she slid her change off the counter, Mr. Morton handed her a peppermint drop.

"Thank you, Mr. Morton," she said, popping the mint into her mouth. Through the glass window she could see a woman crossing the street. It was the neighbor, Mrs. Henks, who had offered to help the Brodskys. By the time Rebecca reached the shop's door, Mrs. Henks was leaning over the buggy, cooing at the baby.

"Why, hello again," the woman said cheerfully. "Looks like you have a way with babies, young lady!"

"Thank you," said Rebecca, pleased. She scanned the street. The boy was nowhere around. The street was bustling on this Sunday morning. Housewives with baskets on their arms stood talking on their apartment steps. A few horses and carts passed by. Two girls called to each other from open windows. An old woman stood on a fire escape, shaking out a rug.

"You must be a favorite with all the mothers in this neighborhood," Mrs. Henks was saying.

"Well, not really," admitted Rebecca. "This is the first time I've taken care of a baby." But now that the baby wasn't crying, she felt quite proud of herself. "I'd be happy to look after your children," she told Mrs. Henks. "I live on the floor above the Brodskys. My name is Rebecca Rubin."

"Why, that's good to know," said Mrs. Henks. "I'm sure I shall ask you one day." They said good-bye, and Rebecca headed home.

When Rebecca reached her building, the dark-haired boy suddenly materialized next to her.

Did he follow me? Rebecca wondered, startled. "Hello," she said cautiously.

He nodded as she parked the buggy at the

stoop and lifted the baby into her arms. "Here, let me help bring buggy inside," he offered.

"Just leave it by the steps, thank you," she said shortly. Who was this boy? He had no business hanging around. She hadn't asked for his help.

The boy stood watching her intently as she went into the building and shut the door.

4
THE GIRL IN THE PARK

Back inside the Rubins' apartment, baby Nora
began fussing more loudly than ever. Rebecca
shook the tin rattle while Mama dabbed ointment
on the baby's rash and pinned on a clean diaper.
Rebecca sang a lullaby in Yiddish that Bubbie
had sung to all her grandchildren: *"Ay-lu-lu,
Ay-lu-lu…"* But even the haunting refrain didn't
calm the crying baby.

Sophie and Sadie had gone to their friend
Lucy's apartment to work on their math lessons.
Benny and Papa had gone to visit Uncle Jacob
and Aunt Fanny in Brooklyn. Victor, however,
was seated at the table. He covered his ears with
his hands. "How can I catch up on my homework with all this noise?" he complained.

Mama wrapped Nora back in her blankets.

THE GIRL IN THE PARK

"Why not take her to the park, Beckie. It's not far, and the fresh air may help calm her down."

"I'll go with her," Victor offered suddenly. "I need some fresh air, too."

"No," Mama replied firmly. "Papa says you may not go out today until all of your homework is done. You have neglected too many assignments, so now you must spend the afternoon studying."

Victor groaned.

"Come back in an hour—sooner, of course, if Nora keeps crying," Mama told Rebecca. "Here, let me pack a lunch to take with you."

Victor glared at Rebecca. She fluttered her fingers in a little wave as she left the apartment with Nora in her arms.

Rebecca settled Nora in the buggy and headed to the park. It was a crisp autumn day, with pale sunshine lighting the brick buildings and rutted streets of Rebecca's neighborhood. As she entered the park, a cool breeze rustled the dry leaves on the trees. Rebecca felt grown up trundling the old buggy along and then sitting on a bench with all the mothers and big sisters, rocking the buggy until Nora finally napped. Now she was enjoying herself! She remembered how she had helped Mama push their buggy to this same park when Benny was a baby.

She opened the grease paper and took out the bread and cheese Mama had given her. As she ate, she looked around at the other children playing in the park. Some were swinging or rolling hoops along the paths, and some were throwing balls on the grass. Some were by the pond, tossing bread to the ducks.

"Save some of your lunch to feed the ducks," said a voice at her side, and Rebecca turned to see a girl standing there—a girl just about her own age with a baby slung on her hip, wrapped in a shawl. The girl licked a dripping ice cream cone. "I am Francesca," she said. "This is my sister, Vincenza. What is your name?"

"I'm Rebecca," she replied. She could tell from the girl's accent that she was not originally from New York City. "Where are you from?"

"I come from Italy," said the girl. "Vincenza, she is born here. She come from America!" Francesca offered Rebecca a bite of her ice cream cone. "You like?"

Tentatively, Rebecca leaned over and licked it. The sweet, cold ice cream melted in her mouth. "It's delicious!"

Francesca beamed. "Go on—you eat the rest."

"Why, thank you!" Rebecca took the dripping cone. In the buggy, Nora started fussing again.

"Is your sister?" asked Francesca, leaning over the buggy.

"Oh, no. I'm just minding her for a while."

Francesca spread out a blanket on the grass and beckoned for Rebecca to join her. Francesca untied the shawl and lowered her baby sister to the blanket. The dark-eyed baby kicked happily and cooed up at her big sister. In the buggy, Nora was crying harder.

"Your baby, she like to play with my sister?" asked Francesca, leaning over the buggy.

"I don't think so," said Rebecca. "She's pretty

fussy. I'd better take her home—oh, wait!" she cautioned as Francesca reached into the buggy and lifted Nora out. Now Nora would probably fuss even more. But no—the Brodskys' baby stared at Francesca, round-eyed, and stopped crying.

"She likes you," said Rebecca.

"I like babies," said Francesca simply, and she laid Nora on the blanket next to Vincenza.

"They look like sisters," Rebecca remarked, admiring the babies' black curls and dark eyes. They were both wearing long white flannel nightgowns. The breeze grew brisk, so she tucked the blanket from Nora's buggy over both infants to keep them warm. "They could almost be twins, like my big sisters—oh!" she broke off as a red ball bounced across the blanket.

Francesca caught it and tossed it to a boy standing by the duck pond with a puppy frolicking at his side. Rebecca glanced at him, and then looked again. Why, it was the same boy she had seen at the shop! Was he following her? But how could he be, when she had just arrived, and he was already playing here?

When he saw Rebecca looking at him, he grinned, and then he turned away and threw the ball into the pond. The puppy dove in and swam to retrieve it.

"You know this boy?" Francesca asked. "Go and play with dog! I watch babies. You go!"

"Oh, no," said Rebecca. "I *don't* know that boy—I just saw him earlier."

There was a silence between the girls as they watched the boy and the puppy at play. With both babies napping peacefully on the blanket, it was pleasant to sit in the autumn sunshine. Rebecca wondered where Francesca lived and was just about to ask when Francesca spoke first.

"I have seven brothers and one sister," she said. "What about you?"

"Seven brothers!" exclaimed Rebecca. "I have only two brothers and two sisters."

"And school? You like?"

"Yes, most of the time," said Rebecca. "Do you like your school?"

"I have nice teacher," said Francesca. "She

helping me learn English. She say I will speak perfect English when I grow up."

"I'm sure you will," Rebecca said warmly. "My cousin Ana hardly knew any English when she came here from Russia, and now she's doing just fine."

"When I grow up," said Francesca, watching the boy with the puppy, "I want to be fine dressmaker, make beautiful clothes."

"I want to be a movie actress," Rebecca confided. Her family always said she had a flair for drama, and once she'd even visited a movie studio and played a small part in a movie. But her parents wanted her to become a teacher.

"I make beautiful costumes for your movies!" Francesca plucked at Rebecca's sleeve. "My neighbor, she is teaching me," she added proudly. Francesca told Rebecca that she hoped soon to be able to make all her own clothes and clothes for everyone in her family. "I practicing every day," she added. "And look here, I sew the *corno* into the hem." She turned up the edge of her skirt to show Rebecca a little hand-stitched animal horn in gold embroidery thread. "Is for a blessing. Against the, how you say? The evil eye—to keep us healthy. Some people wear a corno necklace of gold or silver for good luck, but we—we sell our . . . our *everything* to pay for boat to America. My mama, she say that not matter—a charm of thread is working just as well."

"It's so pretty." Rebecca knew that some Americans carried a rabbit's foot in their pocket for luck. Bubbie said that in Russia people painted intricate designs on eggs to ward off trouble. The Irish had four-leaf clovers. *Maybe Mrs. Brodsky should sew a little Italian blessing onto the hem of Nora's nightgown,* Rebecca thought with a smile. Perhaps that would make the fretful baby stronger and healthier.

Then she remembered Mrs. Brodsky's eyes. She was just about to tell Francesca about poor Mrs. Brodsky, who used to be a dressmaker but could no longer see to sew, when a policeman started walking up the path toward the girls, and Francesca clutched Rebecca's arm.

"Quick!" Francesca hissed. "*Hide!*

5
A DREADFUL MISTAKE

"Why do we need to hide?" Rebecca asked, puzzled. But the policeman approached the girls before Francesca could answer. Rebecca smiled politely when he stopped in front of them. In his arms was the puppy that had been swimming after the red ball. The policeman was young, with a broad freckled face and piercing eyes. Rebecca's smile faded at his stern expression. "Is this your dog?" he asked.

"No, sir," said Rebecca. She glanced around. The boy was no longer in sight.

Francesca flinched. "Dog is ... mine," she whispered.

Rebecca looked at the other girl in surprise. She had assumed the puppy belonged to the boy. Why hadn't Francesca mentioned that the puppy was hers? And why did she look so frightened?

The brisk breeze started blowing harder. "Please see that he stops menacing the ducks," the policeman said brusquely, handing the dog to Francesca. "Put him on a leash!"

Francesca just stared at the ground and didn't reply, so Rebecca spoke up. "We'll keep him with us," she promised.

The policeman nodded and walked off.

Clouds scudded across the sky and the wind blew chill. In the distance, thunder rumbled. A few drops of rain began to fall. The girls turned hurriedly back to the babies on the blanket. Francesca's face was pale.

"I didn't know this was your dog," Rebecca finally said.

"He is pest," said Francesca.

"Why were you afraid of the policeman?" Rebecca pressed. "We weren't doing anything wrong."

"He maybe take me to jail for letting the dog run free."

"Of course he wouldn't! Anyway, the police have more important things to worry about. Like thieves and . . . and kidnappers!"

Thunder boomed overhead, louder now. The puppy squirmed out of Rebecca's arms, pranced over to Nora, and snatched the rattle right out of her hand. Holding it in his mouth by its pink ribbon, he ran off.

"Hey!" Rebecca cried. She tore across the grass after the pup. At the same time the rain began falling hard.

The dog barked happily and bowed low, shaking the rattle. "Give it here!" wheedled Rebecca, dodging this way and that, trying to catch him. Finally she lunged and managed to grab the toy away.

By the time Rebecca returned, Francesca had wrapped the babies in their blankets. Hastily, she tied on their bonnets and settled them into the buggy and the sling, tucking the pink blanket in tightly, then securing the shawl around her shoulder snugly.

"I go home now," Francesca called over the

thunder, as she started running down the path. "Must hurry!" The puppy scampered after her.

"Oh! Good-bye!" called Rebecca. She liked Francesca and hoped they would see each other again soon. It would be fun to bring the babies to the park together, too. Rebecca spread her own wool cape protectively over the buggy to keep Nora dry, wishing she had thought to get her new friend's address.

As Rebecca left the park, two figures darted along the path ahead of her. That boy again— and with him, another boy. Rebecca stopped and squinted. Though the day was darkening and the rain was falling, Rebecca could see that the second boy was her own brother! The boys laughed as they ran, and the larger boy clapped Victor on the shoulder companionably.

Rebecca stared after their retreating figures. *What is Victor doing here? And who is this boy?* He and Victor were obviously friends—and yet she'd never seen or heard of him before today.

Rebecca bent low over the buggy handles, wondering about Victor's friend. Was this boy the bad influence her parents were so worried about? The rain slashed down now in a fierce autumn storm. Nora was well bundled in her blankets and hidden under the cape, but Rebecca herself was dripping wet by the time she arrived at her apartment building.

The building janitor met her at the door and lifted the buggy up the steps.

"Thank you, Mr. Rossi," said Rebecca.

"It's nothing—you help others, I help you," Mr. Rossi replied gruffly.

Rebecca knocked on the Brodskys' door, and Cousin Miriam answered it with a smile. The parlor was still crowded with unpacked trunks, but now a pot of soup bubbled on the stove, filling the apartment with an appetizing aroma.

"You're soaked!" Cousin Miriam exclaimed.

"Yes, but Nora is nice and dry," Rebecca assured her. "She's wrapped up like a little papoose."

Cousin Miriam directed Rebecca to take the baby to Mrs. Brodsky, who lay in the darkened bedroom with a compress over her eyes.

"Ah, thank you," said Mrs. Brodsky, holding out her arms for the baby. "You have been such a help. We couldn't have asked for a nicer welcome to the neighborhood. And just see how quiet and peaceful my Nora is!"

"I was happy to do it," Rebecca told her.

"You're a sweet girl. Do you think you could come again tomorrow after school?" asked Mrs. Brodsky. "If you like, I will speak to your mother about helping on a regular basis. Perhaps we can pay you something. It wouldn't be much, I'm afraid, but a few pennies for the candy store."

Rebecca nodded and agreed to come the next day. It felt good to go home at last to the warmth of her own apartment, where the kitchen smelled of Mama's vegetable soup, and the silver candlesticks on the table gleamed from her sisters' careful polishing. Rebecca smiled. That was one chore she didn't like, while babysitting Nora had turned out to be fun.

"My goodness, you look like you've been for a swim!" exclaimed Mama, taking in Rebecca's wet garments and hair. "Go change into something dry this minute!"

"Where's Victor?" Rebecca asked Mama, hanging her dripping cape on the hook in the kitchen.

"He finished his homework, then offered to go visit Mr. Mendelevich for an hour. I gave him some soup to take along."

Rebecca pressed her lips together and headed for her bedroom. Mr. Mendelevich, a friend of Papa's, had not been well since his wife had passed away in the summer. Victor must have spent only a few minutes with him before he went off to the park with that boy. She remembered the other times recently when Victor had come home late, when he had not been where he was supposed to be or doing what he was supposed to do. What was her brother up to?

❦

At school the next day, Rebecca told her friends about taking care of baby Nora.

"Lucky!" said Rebecca's friend Rose Krensky.

"It's lots of fun. And Mrs. Brodsky may even pay me! If she does, I'll treat you to an ice cream," Rebecca promised. She remembered the delicious ice cream that Francesca had shared with her. Maybe Francesca walked with her baby sister often in the park. Maybe she and Nora would find her there with Vincenza again today.

The day was gray, and rain was falling by the time Rebecca returned home. Would Mrs. Brodsky still want her to take the baby for a walk? She changed out of her school dress, sat at the kitchen table to gobble two of Mama's cinnamon cookies, then hurried downstairs to report for her job.

This time Mrs. Brodsky answered the door herself, the baby in her arms. The young woman's welcoming smile was bright, though her eyes were still red and swollen. Rebecca winced in sympathy.

But how pretty Nora was when her face wasn't all red from crying! "She looks like you when she smiles," Rebecca told Mrs. Brodsky.

"She had a good night's sleep and hasn't been fretful at all today," Mrs. Brodsky told Rebecca contentedly. "Miriam couldn't come to help me, but I was able to cope just fine. You must have had the magic touch, my dear, because since you brought her home, she's been her own sweet self."

Rebecca beamed. "It was fun taking care of her."

"I think it was your outing in the park that calmed her," added Mrs. Brodsky. "I hope you'll take her again. Now, how about giving her a nice bath today? The water is warm. Nora always enjoys her bath!"

Rebecca had helped Mama wash Benny when he was younger, and she remembered it being fun. She placed the washtub on the scrubbed pine table by the stove. She mixed heated water from the stove with cold water from the sink, testing the temperature carefully by dipping her elbow into the bath. She laid out a towel on the kitchen table, then took the baby from Mrs. Brodsky.

"Just sit her up in the bath and hold her firmly," Mrs. Brodsky instructed as Rebecca deftly unwrapped Nora. "I need to put drops in my eyes now," the young mother told Rebecca. "I'll be lying down in the other room. Will you be all right here?"

"We'll be fine," said Rebecca. Nora waved her arms and chuckled as if she agreed.

Now that she was not all red from fussing, Nora had creamy skin and pink cheeks. Rebecca made faces at her as she unpinned the diaper, and the baby laughed. No wonder she was in good humor, thought Rebecca—that salve had done the trick. The rash was completely healed!

So why did Rebecca feel a strange prick of unease?

Nora, who had screamed and fussed when Rebecca unwrapped her the day before, just stared placidly up at Rebecca and pumped her little arms and legs. Rebecca held her carefully and dipped her into the water, bracing for screams—but the baby gurgled with delight.

Rebecca soaped her gently from her neck down to her little toes.

Suddenly she gasped and grabbed the baby's foot. She lifted it out of the water and stared at the pink toes. Mama had just trimmed those tiny nails the day before, but now they were long again! *Of course, nails grow quickly*, she thought. But *so* quickly?

And no diaper rash—how could it be that Nora had healed so completely already?

Rebecca stared into Nora's dark eyes as she rinsed the baby and wrapped her in the towel. She then reached for the pale flannel gown. She diapered and dressed the baby, who gurgled and cooed and smiled up at Rebecca. Nora kicked at the hem of her long gown—the same gown she had been wearing yesterday, Rebecca noticed. There was a flash of yellow.

Rebecca caught her breath. As if in a dream, she turned up the hem of the gown and stared down at an embroidered golden corno. Her eyes widened in horror.

Oh no, oh no, oh no . . . The blood rushed to

Rebecca's face as the terrible truth washed over her. The corno ... for luck ... sewn into all the clothing Francesca made for herself and her family ...

This quiet, happy baby was not Nora at all. This was Francesca's sister, Vincenza!

6
A DESPERATE SEARCH

Rebecca heard a roaring in her ears. She took a deep breath and glanced fearfully through the doorway into the bedroom, where Mrs. Brodsky lay with a folded cloth covering her eyes. Then Rebecca let out her breath slowly and looked back down at the baby—this baby who was somehow the *wrong baby*. The baby looked back calmly, her dark eyes fixed on Rebecca's own.

Mrs. Brodsky stirred on the bed. "Are you finished with the bath, then? Just tuck her here next to me, into her basket, Rebecca dear. We'll both take a little nap."

Rebecca hardly heard her. She just stared numbly down at the baby.

"Oh, and before you go," Mrs. Brodsky was saying, "be sure to wash your hands with the carbolic soap. And would you put the potatoes into the oven to bake? The oven should be hot enough."

Rebecca blinked. "Potatoes," she said blankly. "Yes, of course."

"They're right there on the table. We'll have them for supper when Morris gets home. You really are an enormous help. When my eyes are better, I'll be doing these things myself again."

Rebecca sucked in a ragged breath. *Her eyes are so bad, she hasn't even noticed yet that she's got the wrong baby!* Rebecca knew she had to find the right baby right now—before Mr. Brodsky arrived home.

But wait . . . When he'd come home from work last night, why hadn't Mr. Brodsky realized they had the wrong baby?

The wrong baby, the wrong baby—the words echoed in Rebecca's head. She took a deep, calming breath, trying to hold back the wave of panic that threatened to engulf her. *Oh, of course,* she reasoned. Mr. Brodsky worked an extra job and came home late. Probably the baby had already been asleep. And maybe she was still sleeping when he left for work in the morning. Probably he wasn't around the baby very much anyway, what with working so hard all the time.

Rebecca washed her hands, then wrapped the baby—the baby who wasn't Nora—in a warm blanket. She held her tightly as she went to the big black stove. Two large potatoes sat on top, already well oiled. Automatically, Rebecca picked up a fork in one hand and stabbed each potato, as she had seen Mama do. Then she used a pot holder to open the cast-iron oven door. Holding the baby securely on her hip, she set the potatoes, one by one, on the rack inside. She closed the oven door. They would need an hour to bake. That meant Mr. Brodsky would be home in one hour. She had *one hour* to find Nora.

Rebecca stood in the bedroom doorway. "It's not raining now. I could take . . . the baby . . . for a walk after all," she said, forcing her voice to sound natural.

"A walk? Now?" Mrs. Brodsky removed the cloth from her eyes and slid off the bed. "No,

not after her bath—and in such chilly weather."
She walked to the washstand and poured water
from the jug into the basin. "It'll be getting dark
soon, too. Here, let me wash my hands and I'll
take her. We'll just have a cozy nap together."

"But—" Rebecca began, then pressed her
lips together as Mrs. Brodsky turned and held
out her arms for the baby. There was nothing
Rebecca could do but hand the baby who was
not Nora over to the woman who was not her
mother. Rebecca's stomach churned.

"You're such a help," Mrs. Brodsky said
warmly. "And you have such a way with babies!
She's like a completely different little one today."

Feeling desperate, Rebecca backed out of the
small apartment, shutting the door quietly. She
was dizzy at the thought of what had happened.
Somehow the babies had been switched! She
needed to switch them back immediately! She
would go back to the park alone. She must find
Francesca—*right now.*

Rebecca went upstairs to her own apartment and found Mama and Benny sitting at the table with a snack of bread and jam. "May I go for a walk?" Rebecca asked abruptly.

"In this weather?" asked Mama, looking up. "It's going to rain any moment."

"I'll be back soon—before the rain."

"Well," said Mama, "wear your shawl and take your cape, too."

Rebecca lifted her wool cape off its peg and hurried out the door and down the stairs. She hesitated in the entrance hallway. Should she take the buggy? She would need it to bring Nora home again. But she could run much faster without it. She remembered how Francesca had carried Vincenza in her shawl, fashioned into a sling. Rebecca could make her own shawl serve in the same way.

Rebecca ran all the way to the park. Her thoughts darted all around and back to the inescapable fact that she had taken one baby to the park the day before and returned with another. And she had not noticed until now.

Of course, Francesca's family would have noticed that the fretful baby was not their own Vincenza. They'd probably called the police! Rebecca hoped they *had*—even though she was frightened at the thought of the police coming to her house and maybe even arresting her for kidnapping baby Vincenza. But she and Francesca would explain that somehow they had switched the babies by mistake. They would explain how the puppy had run off with the rattle just as the storm came up, and somehow...somehow things had gotten confused. Perhaps she should go to the police herself; she knew that's what her parents would do. Then Rebecca remembered how frightened Francesca had looked when the policeman spoke to them in the park.

Maybe Francesca would not want her parents to summon the police. Probably Francesca wanted to hide the fact that the babies had been mixed up until she could get her own sister safely back again. Probably Francesca was searching frantically for Rebecca even as Rebecca was searching for her!

If Rebecca and Francesca could find each other at the park, they could switch the babies back this afternoon, right now. Then there would be no harm done!

She dashed along the paths in the park, scanning the bushes, the swings, the grassy area by the pond. She finally stopped at the same place where she'd sat on the grass with the Italian girl. There was no sign anywhere of Francesca.

Rebecca felt the wings of panic beat harder. Little Nora Brodsky was out in New York City ... somewhere, but *where?* Rebecca's footsteps pounded the path—and pounded the truth of the situation into her: *Nora is missing, Nora is missing, Nora is missing!*

Terrified, Rebecca realized she had no idea where to find Francesca. She had no idea where the Italian girl and her family lived. She collapsed onto a park bench to catch her breath. Fear pounded inside her with her pulse.

On the other side of the pond she saw a clutch of boys in a huddle, the tallest one talking earnestly, waving his hands for emphasis. With a start, Rebecca recognized the lanky, dark-haired boy from the shop. And there was Victor, right in the middle of the group!

She hesitated, wary about confronting the boy who was the bad influence on Victor, but then jumped to her feet. He had been playing with Francesca's puppy, after all. He might know her. He might even know where she lived—and where Rebecca could find Nora.

The boy looked over his shoulder and saw Rebecca approaching. Abruptly he broke away from the group. "Hello!" she called. "Maybe you can help me—"

But as she opened her mouth, he ran across the grass, disappearing into a grove of trees.

"Hey! Wait!" she yelled.

Laughing, the other boys darted off, too, glancing back at Rebecca. Victor hesitated and then ran after his pals.

Rebecca raced to catch up with them but stumbled on the dirt path in the grove and nearly fell. Then she came to another park gate. The boys were not in sight.

Why had they run from her?

Rebecca's thoughts were in turmoil. Francesca had walked to the park carrying her baby sister in a shawl, so she *couldn't* live very far away. She had been eating an ice cream cone—so there must be an ice cream parlor somewhere around here. Maybe someone at the ice cream parlor would remember Francesca and know where she lived.

The boys had disappeared. Catching her breath, Rebecca circled the perimeter of the park. She looked down each side street for some sign of Francesca. She asked two men carrying baskets of apples on their shoulders if they knew a girl named Francesca; they shook their heads. She asked a boy selling newspapers, shouting out the headlines, "Police Search City! Kidnappers Still at Large!" He stopped shouting and shrugged. "Nope," he said. "Sorry."

Then Rebecca saw a familiar woman coming out of a shop.

"Mrs. Henks!" called Rebecca, running toward her. If Mrs. Henks shopped in this part of the city, she might know where the ice cream parlors were.

Mrs. Henks stopped and turned around. "Well, hello—" she said, and then put her hand to her forehead. "Oh my! I can't recall your name."

"It's Rebecca. Rebecca Rubin. We met yesterday at the Brodsky's apartment."

"Oh, of course," said Mrs. Henks. She took Rebecca's arm and steered her around the corner. "How nice to see you again." She held up a brown paper parcel tied with string. "I was just shopping. New clothes for my children. They grow so quickly! I'm in quite a hurry, dear... must get home, before the rain."

"Mrs. Henks," Rebecca asked urgently, "do you know where there is an ice cream parlor nearby?"

Mrs. Henks raised her eyebrows. She shook her head. "No, I don't."

"I'm trying to find a girl named Francesca— an Italian girl. All I know is, she bought some ice cream around here. Have you seen her? Do you know her? She's about my age."

Mrs. Henks stared at her impatiently. "Why would I know your friend?"

"Well, I just thought—since you shop in this area . . ."

Mrs. Henks's expression softened. "I'm sorry," she said kindly. "I don't mean to be rude. It's just that I must get home. But let me think."

Rebecca waited, hoping the friendly Mrs. Henks would help.

"An Italian Francesca," said Mrs. Henks musingly. "No, I'm sorry. But look there—across the street. There's Fanelli's Italian Grocery." She pointed to the sign above the shop. "Maybe someone there knows your Francesca."

"Thank you," said Rebecca gratefully. "I'll ask."

Mrs. Henks hurried down the block, her skirts swaying.

Rebecca crossed the street to the Italian grocery. She pulled open the door and a bell jangled. The clerk behind the counter looked up. "How may I help you, little lady?" he asked.

Rebecca asked if he knew a Francesca in the area. He laughed. "I know a lotta Francescas, little lady. Whole lotta Francescas! Which one you need?" The words rolled off his tongue in a lilting Italian accent. "My own daughter, she is Anna-Francesca."

Rebecca brightened. "Is your daughter here?"

His eyes twinkled. "She is sleeping. Is her nap time."

"How old is she? The Francesca I'm looking for is my age."

"No, no. The Francescas I know are not your age. One is old woman. One is beautiful bride. My own Anna-Francesca, my angel, she is three years old."

Rebecca sighed. "Well, what about ice cream parlors?" she asked wearily. "Are there any around here?"

"Oh, lotta ice cream. Closest one is next block, that way. Good luck!"

The late-afternoon air grew colder, and a fine, chilly rain sprinkled down. As Rebecca rounded the corner, she was surprised to see

Mrs. Henks again, hurrying back along the street where Rebecca had first spoken to her. She watched as the woman paused to toss something into the metal trash can on the corner, pressing the lid on tightly before striding away.

It looked to Rebecca as if Mrs. Henks had thrown away the brown-paper parcel she had been carrying home to her children, but of course that wouldn't make any sense. Still, as Rebecca reached the corner, she couldn't resist opening the lid of the trash can for a quick look.

Rebecca wrinkled her nose at the smell of rotting food. There, shoved down among the vegetable scraps and soiled rags, lay the parcel Mrs. Henks had been carrying. Rebecca lifted it out and pulled off the paper. Inside was a small knitted sweater and a pair of matching trousers. The yellow wool was very fine and soft. Imagine throwing out perfectly nice clothes, even if your child had outgrown them!

A man in a bowler hat turned the corner and stopped abruptly, watching Rebecca and fingering his mustache. Her cheeks flushed at the sight of his frown. Embarrassed to be seen digging through the trash, she tucked the yellow sweater and pants under her cape to take home with her. So what if the clothes came from the trash? They were perfectly usable. She would give them to Mrs. Brodsky for Nora.

At the thought of Nora, panic washed over Rebecca again.

She *must* find Nora. She *must* find Francesca.

Without another glance at the disapproving man, Rebecca ran down the street. At the corner, she saw a signboard over a door with words hand-lettered in an ornate script: Martuscelli's Homemade Ices and Gelato. The door was propped open by a barrel of lollipops swirled onto sticks, and Rebecca could see wrought-iron tables and chairs set by the windows. As she stepped into the shop, a burly, balding man behind the soda fountain boomed in a heavy Italian accent, "Welcome to Mar-too-SHELL-ee's! You like ice cream sundae? Or root beer float?"

"No, thank you," said Rebecca with regret. She opened her mouth to ask about Francesca, but before she uttered a word, running footsteps sounded behind her, followed by wild laughter. The man's expression darkened to a scowl. He raised his fist, staring past her. "Get out!" he shouted.

Rebecca wheeled around to see the lanky, dark-haired boy from the park and two other boys—one of them Victor!—grabbing several of the colorful lollipops from the barrel. They raced away, their footsteps pounding the pavement.

"Thieves!" yelled the man. "You boys come back here!"

Victor—a thief? Rebecca's cheeks burned with shame for her brother.

"That Luigi, always up to no good," the man muttered. "Just *pranks*, he says. Always just pranks. But one day he'll go too far, I say. One day it will be jail for him and his crew."

His *crew*. Rebecca bit back the confession that one of those boys was her own brother. Obviously Victor had run off from doing his homework to hang out with his wild friends.

Mama and Papa would be so angry and ashamed if he ended up in jail. Hot fear welled up inside her. She could end up in jail herself if she didn't find baby Nora.

She looked up at the man and cleared her throat several times before she could speak without sobbing. "Ex-excuse me, do you know a girl named Francesca?"

He stared at her. "You mean my own girl, Francesca?"

Another daughter named Francesca? wondered Rebecca. "Well, the Francesca I'm looking for is my age, with long braids and . . . and a baby sister named Vincenza."

The man's angry expression cleared. "*Le mie principesse*, my little princesses," he beamed. "They are my daughters. You can find them at home. We live at number one-fifteen." He leaned over the counter and pointed. "One block down."

"Oh, thank you!" cried Rebecca. She hurried out the door.

The next street was lined with tenement buildings. The tenements looked very much like the one Rebecca's cousin Ana had lived in when her family first came from Russia. As Rebecca slowed to a walk, scrutinizing each building for some sign of Francesca, she heard a familiar bark. There was the puppy, lunging at a cat by the lamppost. The puppy was held in check by a piece of rope around his neck. And there on the bottom step of a front stoop, where the rope was tied to a railing, sat Francesca.

"Francesca!" Her heart glad with relief, Rebecca raced toward the Italian girl.

Francesca was bouncing a little red rubber ball on the sidewalk and scooping up jacks with deft sweeps of her hand. She looked up at Rebecca. "Oh, hello," she said casually. "You come to play?"

7

A TERRIBLE CRIME

"Oh, Francesca!" cried Rebecca, panting. "I've been searching all over. I met your father at the ice cream shop and he told me where to find you!"

"Me, I am glad also," said Francesca. "You are liking jacks?"

"I've come to switch Nora back!"

The other girl stopped bouncing the little red ball. "What are you meaning?" she asked. "Why are you yelling?"

"*Nora!* Where is she?" Rebecca repeated. "We need to switch the babies back!"

Francesca swept up the jacks and ball, stashing them in her pinafore pocket. "I not understand what you are meaning."

"Look," cried Rebecca. "The Brodskys have

your baby! You must have Nora! Where is she?" Rebecca's stomach clenched, and she felt she might be sick.

"Our baby is home with Mama." Francesca gestured down the narrow street.

"But that's *not* your baby!" Rebecca exclaimed. "Surely your mother can tell whether she's got the right baby or not!"

"*Si!* Yes, of course she can tell," said Francesca, frowning fiercely. "We all can tell our own sister. Vincenza is our own baby and no one else's." She untied the dog's rope. "I go to my papa now." She started walking swiftly toward the ice cream shop.

"But there's been a terrible mistake!" Rebecca caught Francesca by the arm. "Go home and look at the baby you have. *Please!* She has a diaper rash! The baby the Brodskys have now doesn't have a rash at all."

"Our baby *does* have rash," said Francesca.

"And Nora's nails are cut short—my mother trimmed them herself—but the baby at the Brodskys' right now doesn't have short nails at all!" How could Francesca not have noticed that her own sister was missing?

"I trim our baby's nails myself, too," Francesca said stolidly. But she wouldn't look at Rebecca.

"Listen, the baby at the Brodskys' is wearing a nightgown with a corno stitched into the hem." How could Rebecca make Francesca believe her? "A corno just like *yours*, Francesca! Mrs. Brodsky can't sew like that anymore, so Nora's gown *can't* have a corno—"

"Yes it can," said Francesca obstinately. "It can and it does." She pulled her arm out of Rebecca's grasp and started running down the street.

"Wait!" Rebecca called desperately.

But Francesca tore around the corner. Rebecca, pelting after her, caught a glimpse of the other girl's long, black-stockinged legs as Francesca crossed the street and dodged around a passing milk cart. Rebecca stopped as the horse and cart rattled past, then looked up and down the street. There was no sign of Francesca. Was she hiding? Where could she have gone so quickly?

"Francesca!" shouted Rebecca desperately.

She ran to the end of the block. Could the girl have gone to her father's ice cream parlor?

She hurried around the corner, but the door of the shop was locked. Rebecca pressed her nose to the glass window but saw no sign of Francesca or her father inside. *Where did she go?*

An alarm seemed to be ringing in Rebecca's head. Her stomach quivered. Her thoughts were so muddled. Nothing made sense. And yet Francesca's father had said that Francesca and Vincenza were his two daughters. Surely a father would know his own baby daughter.

Of course he would! So that meant . . . that *must* mean . . . the baby switch wasn't a mistake. They must have done it on purpose. Both Francesca *and* her father *knew* they had the wrong baby. Perhaps they were hiding inside the ice cream shop right now.

Shaken, Rebecca trudged home through the darkening streets. As she rounded the corner and headed for her apartment, she saw the familiar figure of her friend Rose just coming out the door. "Rose!" she called, and Rose turned around with a smile on her face.

"Oh, I was hoping to see you," she said. "Mama sent me to return some books your papa loaned us. Your mama gave me a cup of tea, and I waited for you, but you didn't come."

"I'm sorry. I wish I could have been home, but—" Her voice broke and her eyes filled with tears.

"Beckie, what is it?" Rose asked, her eyes worried. "What's wrong?"

"Oh, Rose, it's so terrible." Rebecca sank down onto the nearest stoop and put her head in her hands.

Her friend patted her gently on the back. "Tell me."

Rebecca, shivering despite her wool cape, took a deep breath. "Remember how I told you I was taking care of our new neighbors' baby?" she began, and Rose nodded. Biting back tears, Rebecca poured out the whole story.

"So you see," she ended, "I'm desperate to switch the babies back, but Francesca says they weren't switched at all. And now it seems her father is in on it, too. But *why*, Rose? Why would someone steal a baby?"

"For ransom," Rose said.

Rebecca shivered. Could Francesca and her father—and her entire family, maybe—be the same kidnappers that had taken baby Christopher and returned him only the day before?

The girls discussed this possibility in low, intense voices. Maybe the ice cream business wasn't making enough money for the family, and the parents sent Francesca out to steal babies to hold for ransom. Once the ransom was paid, the baby would be dropped off for the police to find and return. Maybe the Brodskys would soon get a ransom note!

But wait—Nora and Vincenza had been *switched*, Rebecca reminded Rose. That was different from a kidnapping, wasn't it? Even if the family wanted to kidnap Nora and hold her for ransom, why would they give their own baby girl, Vincenza, away to a different family?

"Maybe she's not really their baby, either," whispered Rose.

A Terrible Crime

A chill rolled up Rebecca's spine, and she stared at Rose for a long moment. If Vincenza wasn't their baby, then who was she? Rebecca shook her head, trying to think. "There hasn't been any news about a kidnapped baby girl," she reminded Rose.

Rose had another suggestion. "I once read a story about a baby who died, and the poor, grieving mother lost her mind and tried to steal someone else's baby to replace her own. Maybe that's why Francesca's family has stolen Nora. Maybe that's why they won't admit she isn't their baby!"

"But neither baby is dead," Rebecca pointed out. "I saw them both at the park, completely alive! So the real question is, why would someone switch babies at all?"

"Well," said Rose, "maybe to get a better one. A healthy one. Maybe if their baby was sick, they would switch it for a healthy baby."

But Rebecca shook her head. That was the perplexing thing: the fussy baby with diaper rash was the one that Francesca took, leaving the Brodskys with a contented, happy baby.

Rose considered this. "Well, my bubbie said she knew her babies were healthy if they had a good strong pair of lungs. So maybe both babies are healthy after all, even the fussy one."

If the fussy baby was the healthy one...Stunned, Rebecca stared at Rose. She pictured the calm face of the quiet baby in Mrs. Brodsky's arms. "Rose, oh, no," she breathed. "I think I know why Francesca switched babies. And her parents must be in on it, too, because of course they'd have to know."

"Know what?" demanded Rose. "Rebecca, you are scaring me!"

"They would have to know something is terribly wrong with their baby."

The girls stared at each other. "I don't understand," said Rose. "You mean the *quiet* baby is the sick one?"

Rebecca took a deep breath. It was hard work, trying to make sense of a situation that didn't make any sense. But she had to figure it out. There would be no way to get Nora back until she understood why Nora had been taken. "Imagine you had a baby," she said quietly. "Imagine your baby got sick, and grew weak, and quiet, and listless. Maybe the doctor even told you it was going to die."

Rose put her hands to her cheeks. "I remember a girl, Malka, from the Old Country—that exact thing happened to her. Her brother died before his first birthday. It was so sad. He grew so quiet, he could hardly move—and though the doctor tried his best, no one could save him."

"It's dreadfully sad." Rebecca's thoughts were racing. "It's so sad, a family might not be able to bear it. If Francesca's baby sister had the same sort of disease, she'd be quiet and still. Maybe when Francesca saw Nora at the park, fussing and crying, she thought, *Now there's a healthy baby with good, strong lungs!* And so she just—"

"*Switched* her?" finished Rose, eyes widening. "That's awful."

"It's a terrible crime," agreed Rebecca. "It's a different kind of kidnapping."

Rebecca felt frightened and drained. Still,

talking to Rose had helped to calm her down. "I'd better go in now," she said, giving her friend a hug. "But thank you, Rose. I'm going to tell my parents what has happened."

Rose nodded gravely. "It's the best thing to do."

Rebecca said good-bye and went inside the apartment building with new resolve. Her heart sank at the sight of Nora's empty buggy in the hallway. Had Mr. Brodsky come home from work yet? If he had, then he must have noticed that the baby in his wife's arms was not his own Nora. Rebecca removed the little yellow sweater and knitted pants from her cape and tucked them under the pillow in the buggy. She could not face the Brodskys now.

With a shaking hand, Rebecca opened the door of her own apartment and stepped inside.

8
Trouble at Home

"There you are, Beckie!" Sophie said.

"Mama is worried you're starting to act like Victor," Sadie added.

"I'm sorry," Rebecca mumbled. "It only just got dark."

Mama came in from the kitchen, her cheeks red from the heat. "Beckie!" she said. "Surely you haven't been out walking all this time."

"I met up with Rose," Rebecca replied. "We were just talking."

"Well, come in and get warmed up." Mama touched Rebecca's cold cheek and took her cape, hanging it on a peg. "Come drink some tea."

"Thank you, Mama," Rebecca said, accepting the hot drink gratefully. But she couldn't allow herself to be comforted. Too much was wrong.

"Mama, I need to talk to you and Papa."

"Papa is having a talk with your brother just now," Mama said with a sharp glance toward the bedroom.

At least that meant Victor was home again, thought Rebecca. She sat down on the couch and sipped the tea.

"Papa is upset that Victor went out after school with his friends instead of coming home to do his homework," Sophie whispered after Mama returned to the kitchen.

"Papa is *furious,* you mean," Sadie said.

"Well, he had told Victor to come straight home to build the sukkah," Sophie clarified. "Benny was here, waiting and waiting."

Rebecca's head was so full of her own troubles, she had forgotten all about the sukkah. Her family loved Sukkos, the week when Jews mark the autumn harvest time. It was great fun to build a sukkah shelter and eat all their meals in it during that special week. Usually they built the shelter in the small yard behind the apartment building. This year Benny had begged to set it up on the rooftop, and Victor had said he would build it there and Benny could help. Together the brothers were planning to erect a three-sided wooden frame and lay fresh leafy branches across the top for the roof.

Benny sat on the floor now, sketching pictures of how he wanted their sukkah to look. She could tell by his slumped shoulders that her little brother was sorely disappointed.

Rebecca heard Papa open the bedroom door. "I asked that you come home and finish your schoolwork, but you did not," she overheard him say to Victor. "I asked that you start building the sukkah, and yet you did not. You must stay in the bedroom with no dinner."

Papa's heavy footsteps sounded through the kitchen. He came into the parlor, settled in his armchair, and picked up the evening newspaper. Mama followed, wiping her hands on her apron.

"Victor probably filled up on ice cream already," Sadie said. "And those boys he's become friends with! The ringleader is an

Italian boy named Luigi."

"I heard that boy has been stopped by the police for stealing," Sophie said in a low voice.

Benny looked up from his sketch with wide eyes. "Will he go to jail?" he asked.

Sophie remained ominously silent, but Sadie spoke up. "He will if he's bad enough."

Benny's lip trembled. "I don't want Victor to go to jail!" he wailed, as Mama gave Sadie a stern look.

"Nor do we," said Sophie, reaching out to ruffle Benny's hair. "And he won't if he stays out of bad company."

"All right, girls, that's enough," said Mama with a sigh. "Please set the table." Then she turned to Rebecca. "Now, what was it you wanted to talk to me about, Beckie?"

Rebecca set down her teacup. "Well," she began, but just then Papa rustled his newspaper.

"More bad news," he said. "There's been another kidnapping."

Everyone wanted to hear the details, so Papa read the article aloud.

Second Kidnapping Stuns New Yorkers

Seven-month-old Richard Griffin was stolen away when his fifteen-year-old sister, Margaret, left his buggy outside Hewlitt's Millinery Shop, where she was picking up a new hat for their mother. When the girl left the shop, the buggy was empty, and a ransom note had been left in place of the baby. The panicked girl ran back into the shop, and Mr. George Hewlitt, the owner, telephoned for the police. Officers arrived promptly but could find no trace of the baby.

As in the case of six-month-old Christopher Porter, who was returned safely Saturday night, $100 is demanded by the kidnappers. But the stricken parents say they do not know how they will come up with the ransom money. They plead for the safe return of their beloved son. "My poor baby," the tearful mother lamented to reporters. "I pray they do not harm my little boy!"

Anyone who may have information regarding this case is urged to come forward immediately.

"Such a nightmare for the family," said Mama softly, resting her hand on Benny's head. "How do they bear it?"

Rebecca shivered. So many things going

wrong, and all to do with babies. Resolutely, she stood up. "Mama, may we please talk in my bedroom?"

The urgency in Rebecca's voice made Mrs. Rubin clasp her hands together. "Goodness, yes. Come with me—I'll just turn down the soup so it doesn't burn." She hurried into the kitchen, and Rebecca followed.

Inside the girls' bedroom, Mama closed the door and put her hands on Rebecca's shoulders. "What is it, Beckie?"

"Something awful!" whispered Rebecca urgently. "Nora is missing!" At Mama's gasp, Rebecca poured out the whole story. She told Mama about meeting Francesca in the park, and how she realized the babies had been switched, and how she and Rose figured out that the Brodskys must now have a sick baby who wasn't even their own. "The baby may even be dying," she whispered, clasping her hands in front of her to keep them from trembling. "We have to call the police!"

As she listened, Mama's eyes widened. But

when Rebecca finished, Mama smiled kindly. "Oh, Beckie," she said. "At first I thought you were making up one of your dramatic stories. You're a talented actress, I know, but I do believe you really think what you're saying is the truth."

Rebecca stared at Mama, shocked. "Of course I believe it. This is *serious*."

Her mother shook her head. "But Beckie, I just saw Mr. Brodsky this morning when he was leaving for work. He didn't seem the least bit worried about anything except his wife's poor eyes."

Rebecca swallowed hard. "I'm not lying," she mumbled.

"Of course not," Mrs. Rubin exclaimed. "I know that. But if the Brodskys thought for one single minute that they didn't have the right baby, they would have gone to the police immediately." She encircled Rebecca's shoulders and gave her a hug. "Why, I never even got our twins switched around, though you know how people always say that Sadie and Sophie are as alike as two peas in a pod!"

"This is different, Mama—"

"A mother always knows her own child," Mama said gently. "I can see that you are worried, but I'm sure there's no reason to be." She gave Rebecca a hug. "Come eat dinner now. I've made your favorite noodles for the soup."

A mother always knows her own child. Rebecca wanted to believe Mama. "But Mrs. Brodsky is nearly blind, Mama."

"Now, Beckie," Mama said, "please don't bother Mrs. Brodsky. That poor woman has enough to cope with. And Papa and I have enough to worry about just now with Victor's behavior. Let's have no more talk of stolen babies and terrible illnesses. Your lively imagination is getting the best of you."

Returning to the kitchen, Rebecca trailed wordlessly behind Mama. While Mama served the noodles and soup, Benny ran to call the twins and Papa to the table. Rebecca sat, her cheeks burning. She felt as if she were coming down with a fever. *Mrs. Brodsky can't see that she's got the wrong baby! And Mr. Brodsky works so much, he doesn't even know what his own baby looks like. So now they've got a sick baby, while Francesca's family has their healthy Nora. And Mama thinks I'm making up a story!*

Victor remained in Mama and Papa's bedroom until supper was finished, emerging when Papa called him. He walked through the kitchen to the parlor without looking at his sisters and brother. Rebecca could see him standing stoically by the big armchair while Papa and Mama reminded him of his responsibilities.

"You promised to come home to study and to help Benny build the sukkah," she heard Papa say. "But look at you. Running wild with ruffians. Never studying. And now disappointing people who are counting on you." Papa's voice was severe. "Let me remind you that we are, each of us, known by the company we keep." From the kitchen, Rebecca heard Papa's heavy sigh. She could imagine Mama's troubled face as Papa added, "A good education, my son, is the ticket to a good future in this country. It is one reason we came to America, the chance for you to get an education. Do not throw it away."

"Yes, Papa," said Victor. "I'm sorry, Mama." He came into the kitchen and sank into a chair at the table across from Benny, looking quietly ashamed.

"Are you going to run away to sea?" asked Benny, breaking the silence. "Like a pirate? Because if you do, I want to come with you. But if you stay, then you ought to help build the sukkah on the roof, because you *promised!*"

Victor sighed heavily. "All right, let's go be pirates."

Rebecca and her sisters listened wordlessly as they cleared the table and washed the dishes. As Rebecca dried the soup bowls, she pictured Victor racing out of the ice cream shop with his stolen candy. *One day it will be jail for him and his crew,* Mr. Martuscelli had said.

Rebecca remembered how Francesca had feared the policeman in the park. She'd claimed to be worried about jail for having a dog off the leash, but probably the Italian girl was worrying about a far greater crime than that. Anyone who stole babies would end up in jail for a long time—longer than someone who stole candy.

Her thoughts in turmoil, Rebecca drifted into her chair at the table. She could hear her parents in the parlor, talking in low voices. The twins and Benny left the kitchen, but Rebecca and Victor stayed at the table.

Victor opened his math book and started writing out equations.

"I saw you and your friend stealing those lollipops," Rebecca whispered across the table.

He looked up sharply.

"At Martuscelli's ice cream parlor. I saw you. Mr. Martuscelli called you *thieves!*"

Victor glared at her. "I am not a thief!"

"I know what I saw," she muttered. "You shouldn't hang out with that boy Luigi. He's trouble!"

"You don't know him," Victor hissed. "We didn't steal anything, so stay out of my business!"

Rebecca brought her homework to the table

but found it impossible to concentrate. She had never known her brother to lie. And yet she had seen him take the lollipops. Francesca was lying, too, when she said the baby at her house was Vincenza.

Rebecca's stomach clenched at the thought of baby Nora out there in the great city somewhere, without her real mother or father to protect her.

And it was her fault. She was the one who had not kept Nora safe.

9

KIDNAPPER ON THE LOOSE

Rebecca dreamed that night of a baby buggy careening down a steep, grassy hill. Desperately she tried to stop it from plunging over the cliff. Somehow she grabbed the blanket-wrapped bundle just as the buggy fell over the side, only to find that she was clutching a bundle of clothes instead of a baby—

She gasped and awoke. Heart pounding, she lay in bed, trying to erase the awful image of that falling buggy from her mind, when a scraping sound made her stiffen.

She recalled Victor's dirt-stained nightshirt. Had he sneaked out again to run wild with Luigi? Taking a deep breath, Rebecca slid out of bed and crept through the kitchen to the front parlor.

Benny was sound asleep, with the stuffed bear Bubbie had made for him tucked into the crook of his elbow. Victor was a big lump on the couch. He had pulled the quilt all the way over his head.

So, if Victor had not made the noise, who had? Rebecca stared harder at the lump on the couch. With a growing sense of suspicion, she crossed the room and poked Victor. But the lump on the couch was not her brother at all, only his pillows.

Victor was gone.

Papa always locked and bolted the door before he went to bed. Rebecca tiptoed to the door now. Sure enough, the bolt had been slid back. That was the scraping sound Rebecca had heard. Glancing over at Benny, she turned the knob. The door opened easily. Rebecca peered into the dark hallway. Victor had run out into the New York City night—but why? What was he up to with Luigi's gang?

Not just stealing lollipops. The shops were closed at night.

Rebecca closed the door, leaving it unlocked. Of course she should tell her parents—and yet she hesitated. She hated to add to Papa's and Mama's worries. She went back to bed and lay waiting, strung as tightly as a fiddle string. At last, an hour later, she heard the click of the door, reassuring her that her brother had come home.

That's the main thing, she thought. *He's home.*

But it was a long time before sleep would come.

❧

In the morning when Rebecca came to the breakfast table, Victor was bent over his bowl of oatmeal. He scraped the bowl clean and handed it to Mama for a second helping.

Papa rustled the newspaper, turning pages.

"It's good news," Sadie told Rebecca as she pulled out her chair and sat down.

"Indeed it is," agreed Mama. "But somebody's found a lucrative business."

"What do you mean?" Rebecca asked. Papa tapped the newspaper lying open on the table in front of her. She gasped. "The second kidnapped baby has been returned. Look at this!"

Ransomed Baby Returned Safely

Little Richard Griffin was found safe last night on the steps of the New York Public Library on Fifth Avenue, many miles from the millinery shop from which he was taken, after caring neighbors raised the $100 ransom demanded by the kidnappers. The infant boy was found wearing unfamiliar clothing, and his fair curls had been cut short and were blackened with soot.

The unknown kidnapper remains at large. Anyone with information is urged to contact the nearest police station. Police presence on the streets has been increased throughout the city, but parents are cautioned not to leave their children unattended.

"At least he was unharmed," Mama said, setting a bowl of oatmeal in front of Benny. "That's what matters most."

"It's good news indeed," said Papa. "Rebecca, I'd like you to walk Benny to school today, just to be safe."

"I can walk by myself!" Benny protested. "I'm not like a baby, left outside a shop!"

Rebecca remembered how Luigi had lingered over baby Nora—the real baby Nora—outside the pharmacy on Sunday. *What if* ... Rebecca hardly dared form the thought. She shot Victor a sharp look, but her brother did not look up from his breakfast.

What if Luigi was the kidnapper of the two little boys? He would require a helper—for surely it would take at least two people to organize snatching the babies, caring for them somewhere till the ransom money was paid, and then collecting the ransom, while at the same time, in another part of the city, the babies were left for people to find. Luigi would need an accomplice. And he and Victor were in the same gang. And Victor was sneaking out at night. Could her brother possibly be involved with the kidnappings?

Worry ticked inside Rebecca like a heartbeat.

❦

All that day at school, Rebecca could not concentrate. She fretted about her brother and anguished about the switched babies—Nora, who had been stolen, and Vincenza, who was ill. She sat at her desk, but the teacher might have been speaking Italian for all Rebecca could understand of her lessons. When asked for the answer to a math problem, Rebecca just stared blankly while the teacher tapped her foot. When asked to name the largest continent, Rebecca blinked vaguely while the class tittered.

"You're lucky not to have been kept after school," said Rose as the class filed out of school at the end of the day.

"I have to get the babies switched back, Rose. *I have to!* Will you come with me?"

Rose hesitated only a moment. "Yes—but let me tell my sister so my mother won't worry."

Rebecca waited impatiently while Rose located her older sister at the school gate, and then the two girls ran to Rebecca's apartment. Rebecca was determined to take the Brodskys' baby—*the imposter*—back to Francesca's apartment this very afternoon. This time she would go to the door and force her way inside. She would *make* them switch the babies back.

Rebecca knocked firmly on the Brodskys' apartment door. Cousin Miriam opened it and smiled at Rebecca and Rose. "Hello, girls. What can I do for you?"

"Hello," said Rebecca. "My friend Rose and I would like to take Nora out for a walk." She looked past Cousin Miriam to Mrs. Brodsky, who was holding the baby. Mrs. Brodsky was wearing a hat and looked dressed to go out. The baby chortled, waving her little hands.

"Is that you, Rebecca?" asked Mrs. Brodsky, peering over the baby's head. "I thought I recognized your voice. And this is your friend?"

Rebecca introduced Rose.

"It's good of you to stop by, and I hope you'll come again—perhaps tomorrow? Mr. Brodsky is taking me to the doctor, and Cousin Miriam will look after Nora." She smiled gratefully. "We are fortunate to live so close to my husband's cousins now. We hardly ever saw them before we moved here."

Mrs. Brodsky kissed the top of the baby's head and gently passed her to Cousin Miriam. "Morris should be home any minute," she said and turned away. "Now, where did I put my shawl?"

"Oh, please, let us take the baby for a walk," Rebecca begged Cousin Miriam in a low voice. "We'll look after her!"

"Not today, dear," she replied. "I took her out already, just after lunch. Thank you anyway." She smiled at them as she shut the door.

Tears smarted behind Rebecca's eyes as she turned away. She saw Mr. Brodsky entering the building. Cousin Miriam didn't know Nora, but now Mr. Brodsky would see, she thought. *It's broad daylight, and he can't help but see it's the wrong baby!*

10
MIDNIGHT ENCOUNTER

"Hello, Rebecca," Mr. Brodsky said easily as he stepped inside the apartment building. "Have you and your friend just come home from school?"

"Yes," she said. "Rose and I wanted to take Nora to the park."

"Ah, check with Cousin Miriam about that. My wife and I are off to the doctor. He has some new eyedrops he'd like her to try." As he spoke, he opened the door to the apartment. "I had to leave work early. Luckily my boss understands." He waved and shut the door.

Rebecca remembered her parents talking about Mr. Brodsky's having to work two jobs. She knew that he left early in the morning, probably before the baby woke up, and came home late at night, probably when the baby was asleep. Rebecca braced herself now for the shouts and screams that were bound to come when he realized his wife was holding the wrong baby. She clutched Rose's arm. "Wait till he sees the baby isn't Nora!"

But there were no screams, and after another moment the Brodskys' door opened and Mr. and Mrs. Brodsky stepped out into the hallway. He held her arm protectively and guided her steps.

"Hello again, girls," he said.

Why didn't you notice it's the wrong baby? The thought hammered in Rebecca's head, though she smiled weakly at the Brodskys. "We're just on our way up," she murmured, and she started up the stairs to her own apartment with Rose behind her.

Rose nudged Rebecca's arm. "This doesn't make sense."

Rebecca felt a surge of gratitude for Rose, who was the only person who seemed to understand the terrible situation. Her worry raged like a fever, and her cheeks were flushed as the girls entered the apartment.

Bubbie sat at the table with Mama. The women were peeling potatoes and drinking hot tea. "Home already!" said Bubbie. "You must be running all the way. Hello, Rose."

"Hello," Rose said shyly.

Rebecca hung up their coats and kissed her grandmother and mother. "We just saw the Brodskys. Mr. Brodsky came home early to take Mrs. Brodsky to the doctor. I wanted to look after the baby, but their cousin is there already." Her voice trembled. "Mama, I just don't see why nobody notices that that baby isn't the same!"

She saw Mama and Bubbie exchange a troubled glance. "Have a snack," Mama suggested soothingly, lifting the teapot to pour some fragrant tea into two china cups. "Sit down, girls." She buttered thick slices of bread and set them in front of Rebecca and Rose.

"You are still telling this story?" Bubbie asked gently. "Your friend, she has heard the story, too?"

"Beckie has such a flair for storytelling,"

Mama sighed. At the same time Rebecca insisted, "It's the truth!"

Rose looked uncomfortable. "I believe Rebecca. I think something very strange has happened with the babies."

Rebecca gave her friend a grateful look.

Just then the door burst open and Benny tumbled in, followed by Sophie and Sadie. "Victor has to stay after school!" Benny announced. "He got in *trouble*."

The twins explained that Victor's teacher had given him detention for not turning in his homework. "He has to clean all the erasers," said Sophie. "It'll take ages!"

"And he'll come crawling home through dark streets around midnight," added Sadie, "leaving trails of chalk dust."

"You girls are as melodramatic as Rebecca," Mama said disapprovingly over the twins' laughter.

Rebecca felt that Mama was terribly unfair. She sat stonily while her sisters and Benny ate their snacks and left the table. In the chair next to Rebecca, Rose nibbled her bread and remained silent. Mama took the pot of potatoes to the stove and began preparations for dinner.

Bubbie reached over and patted Rebecca's hand. "That Victor," she said, shaking her head. "A trial to his parents. Not like you, Rebecca." Bubbie turned to Rose. "You have brothers, Rose? You know how important it is for boys to get good grades in school?"

"Just one sister," Rose replied politely. "But my parents always say we must study hard."

"Girls need good grades, too," Mama said from the stove. "Especially if they're going to become teachers." Mama looked pointedly at Rebecca.

"What if they want to become actresses?" asked Rebecca in a quiet voice.

Mama shook her head. "A lady doesn't make a display of herself."

Rebecca sighed. Rose gave her a sympathetic look.

"But do not forget Queen Esther in the Bible," said Bubbie, unexpectedly arguing with Mama.

"She is fine lady, but strong and courageous, too. She is not sitting meekly when danger comes."

Rebecca knew the story of how Queen Esther had risked her life to speak to the king and save the lives of the Jews. She smiled at her grandmother.

"A lady is bold when she needs to be," said Bubbie.

❧

Late that night Rebecca lay awake. The apartment was so quiet, she could hear the clock ticking on the mantle in the parlor. All the Rubins were asleep. *Or maybe not all*, Rebecca thought, frowning as she heard once again the telltale scraping of the bolt on the door.

Rebecca swung her legs over the side of her bed. She left the room, tiptoeing carefully so as not to wake her sisters. In the parlor Benny slept soundly, and Victor's couch was again piled with pillows. She walked to the window and looked down at the empty street.

Where was Victor going? Should she follow him? She opened the apartment door and slipped into the dark hallway. She crept down the stairs, feeling a pang at the sight of Nora's buggy in the shadows. She cracked opened the heavy front door of the building and peeked out at the street, hoping that Mr. Rossi would not hear her.

A fine rain was falling. A few lights were glowing in windows across the street, but most of the buildings were dark.

Then Rebecca heard footsteps ringing on the asphalt. She peered through the crack and saw the hunched figure of a woman hurrying down the street, her head protected from the rain by a shawl, lugging a large basket over one arm. Recognition pricked at the back of Rebecca's mind.

Out of the shadows another figure materialized. A man in a bowler hat strode across the street and spoke to the woman. She waved her free hand, seeming agitated. After a moment he reached for the basket. Rebecca strained to see in the darkness. Quickly they walked across the street, the man's hand on the woman's arm, and they vanished together into the shadows between the two buildings.

Had the woman gone with him willingly? Or had she been forced? Uneasily, Rebecca waited another few minutes, but the man and woman did not reappear. Nor did Victor.

From the doorway, Rebecca could see something was lying on the sidewalk, forming a little mound. Was it something that had fallen from the basket? It looked small. Perhaps a sock . . .

Rebecca darted into the rain. She scooped up the damp cloth, shook it out, and saw it was a bonnet—a very small, lacy white bonnet embroidered with tiny bluebells, now soiled from the wet pavement. Perhaps the woman had been carrying laundry in her basket and the bonnet had dropped out. Or perhaps it had fallen earlier and belonged to Nora or another baby in the neighborhood. Rebecca pushed the front door closed and headed for the stairs. She would wash and dry the bonnet and then give it to the Brodskys, good as new.

If only she could give them their baby as easily.

Rebecca sighed. She didn't know how to find Nora, and she didn't know where to search for Victor. Wearily, she climbed the stairs. She was just opening the door to her apartment when a faint noise above her head startled her. She heard the soft pad of footsteps on the stairs.

Someone was coming down!

Could Bubbie or Grandpa be up so late? Had one of them taken ill and needed help from Rebecca's parents? What would they say if they saw Rebecca out of bed this late? But Bubbie and Grandpa would not come down the stairs so stealthily, like thieves in the night. Holding her breath, Rebecca slipped into her apartment and shut the door quietly. She slid the bolt.

The footsteps in the hallway stopped. She was sure someone was right on the other side of the door. She could almost hear the person breathing. She clenched the damp bonnet tightly and watched as, slowly, the doorknob started to turn.

11
UP TO NO GOOD?

The doorknob turned to the left. It turned to the right. Suddenly it rattled vigorously. Rebecca jerked backward, covering her mouth with her hand to stifle her scream. A small whimper escaped her lips.

"Beckie?" The voice was low but clear. It came through the keyhole. "Beckie, is that you?"

Rebecca let out her breath. She was shaking. "*Victor!*" she whispered, and slid open the bolt.

Victor opened the door and stepped quickly inside. He was wearing his white nightshirt stuffed into a pair of old trousers. "Beckie!" he breathed when he'd entered the apartment and slid the bolt again. "You frightened me!"

"You frightened *me!*" But, oh, she was glad to see him!

"What are you doing out of bed?" he hissed. "If Papa and Mama knew..."

Rebecca gasped. "You're a fine one to talk! You're lucky I didn't tell them you were gone. You're lucky I didn't call the police."

He looked puzzled rather than frightened. "Why would you call the police?"

She countered with another question. "What were you doing out there?"

Victor stared at his sister. "Nothing that would interest the police!"

Rebecca's voice trembled. "It's bad enough that you've been hanging out with that boy Luigi, and that you're stealing and sneaking out at night. But *kidnapping?*"

"*What?*" Victor took her arm and steered her to the couch. "You think I'm a *kidnapper?* Are you crazy?"

Whispering so as not to waken Benny, Rebecca ticked off her evidence. She told Victor how Luigi had paid so much attention to Nora. She described how Luigi had run away when the policeman came into the park. She had seen

Luigi—and Victor—stealing candy. "The ice cream man told me Luigi's been up to no good, always getting into trouble, him and his crowd. And you're in his crowd, Victor! You're running wild with him, just as Papa and Mama said. And you've been sneaking out at night—on the *very same nights* the kidnapped babies were returned!"

Victor batted her on the head with his pillow. "You're a terrible detective. And Mama is right, you make everything into a melodrama! Listen, Rebecca." He lowered his voice so that she had to lean close to hear. "I admit I've been hanging around with Luigi. He's good fun. And yes, I've joined him in playing a few pranks, but that's all."

"Pranks?" Her voice was dubious.

"Pranks—like pulling laundry from clothes-lines and making a scarecrow out of all the clothes. Like gluing pennies to the sidewalk and watching people try to pick them up." Victor chuckled and then earnestly looked into her eyes. "Luigi's a good guy. He's harmless."

"Stealing isn't harmless."

He sighed. "Luigi was just giving his papa a hard time. Mr. Martuscelli didn't think of it as stealing. He didn't call the police, did he?"

Mr. Martuscelli was Luigi's . . . papa?

"Look, I'm tired," Victor was saying quietly, pulling off his cap. "Let's get to bed." He put his hand on her shoulder. "And Beckie? Stop suspecting me of every crime in the city. I'm your brother, for goodness' sake!"

Rebecca hardly heard him. If Mr. Martuscelli was Luigi's papa, that meant *Luigi and Francesca were brother and sister!*

Rebecca stood up abruptly. The connection between Luigi and Francesca made Rebecca all the more certain that the Martuscelli family was up to no good. Her thoughts were racing. She jabbed her finger into Victor's chest. "All right. If you're not in Luigi's kidnapping gang, then what *were* you doing sneaking out tonight?"

He looked at her soberly for a long minute. "I'm not going to tell you—yet. You'll find out soon enough."

12
SHOWDOWN!

The next morning Rebecca jumped out of bed, resolved to confront the Martuscelli family. Her own family might think she was melodramatic, always telling stories, and her brother might accuse her of imagining crimes, but he was definitely keeping something a secret, and she didn't know if she could trust him. The one thing she knew for certain was that she had not imagined the baby switch.

The minute school let out, Rebecca ran home and knocked on the Brodskys' apartment door.

"Rebecca, is that you?" asked Mrs. Brodsky, opening the door and peering through swollen eyelids. "Come in, dear."

"Hello," said Rebecca, stepping carefully past Mrs. Brodsky into the dimness of the apartment. A cheerful chortle sounded from the large basket in the center of the table, and little hands waved in the air. *She's so peaceful, so calm*, thought Rebecca, looking down at the soft dark hair and flushed cheeks. *Such pink cheeks*. Did the baby have a fever?

"Mrs. Brodsky, it's not too cold today, and the sun is shining. Please may I take . . . the baby"—Rebecca couldn't bear to call her Nora when she knew it wasn't Nora at all—"to the park?"

"Why, I'm sure she'd love an outing," said Mrs. Brodsky. "I've already fed her, and she's had a good nap. A short walk should be fine, as long as you keep her bundled up."

"Oh, thank you!" Swiftly, Rebecca lifted the baby out of the basket and smiled at her. "Come on, little one. Let's get you ready!" She tied on her bonnet, swaddled the baby in two blankets, and then picked her up and headed for the door.

Rebecca decided she would go through the park and look for a policeman. With the kidnappers still on the loose, there would be policemen all over the city. When she found one, she would tell him about the switch, and he would go to Francesca's house and make her switch the babies back. Then he would arrest her and Luigi—and their criminal parents. Justice would be done, and all would be right again.

But first she stopped at her own apartment to tell Mama she was taking the baby out.

"Beckie, I'm not sure it's a good idea." Mama's expression was clouded.

Rebecca stood in the doorway, desperate to be on her way.

"There's been another kidnapping." Mama's voice caught in her throat. "And this time right here in our own neighborhood—outside Morton's Pharmacy! When I think of those poor parents..." Mama shook her head.

Rebecca's heart sank. "Papa didn't read about it to us this morning."

"I heard about it from the butcher. It will probably be in the afternoon paper. A little girl this time, that's all I know. So I'd rather not have *my* little girl wandering the streets—and with a baby, too!"

"Mama, *please*. The other babies were taken when someone left them alone. I won't leave the baby alone for one second! Mrs. Brodsky herself thought it was fine. Please, Mama!"

Mama hesitated. "I wonder if Mrs. Brodsky has heard about this latest kidnapping." She sighed. "Well, you're a big girl. All right—just to the park and then straight back."

"Thank you, Mama." Rebecca hugged her mother.

Then Mama came out into the hallway to help Rebecca get the buggy out the door to the sidewalk. "Hello, Nora, sweet darling," Mama cooed at the baby.

Rebecca pressed her lips together. And as soon as Mama went back inside, she ran with the buggy as fast as she dared, jolting along the pavement. The baby laughed with each bump, and Rebecca felt a prick of tears at the sound. She was a sweet darling, but she wasn't Nora. She was Vincenza Martuscelli.

Who would take care of baby Vincenza if her family went to prison? A sick baby would need a good nurse. *Maybe Mama will help,* Rebecca thought. Maybe the baby could even live with the Rubins.

Rebecca reached the park and slowed to a walk. She looked left and right as she followed the path, but there was no sign of the young policeman, or of any police officers at all. *You'd think with kidnappers lurking, there would be police all around!* she thought. But maybe the police were undercover, blending in with ordinary New Yorkers.

She saw people she knew, but couldn't stop to greet them. Old Mr. Mendelevich walked haltingly, arm in arm with his daughter. Mrs. Henks strolled past the fountain with a man in a bowler hat at her side. The man gave Rebecca a piercing glance, and she flushed in embarrassment, recognizing him as the man who had watched her rooting through the trash. But wait—wasn't he also the man she'd seen the night before in the dark street, the man who had taken the basket and hurried the woman away? No wonder the woman had seemed familiar!

She was their neighbor.

Mrs. Henks beckoned to her now, but Rebecca did not have time to chat. She bent over the buggy and pushed swiftly onward and out of the park, jogging to the neighborhood where she had seen Francesca playing jacks. There was no sign of the girl. But a black-haired woman in a tattered shawl sat on the stoop where Francesca had played. She was reading a newspaper while bouncing a baby on her knee. And the baby was fussing.

Nora!

Rebecca stopped and stared at the baby. She wrapped her arms around herself to stop her sudden trembling. Taking a deep breath, she set the brake on the buggy at the foot of the steps.

"Hello," she called. Despite her best efforts, she couldn't manage to keep an accusing tone out of her voice. "Is that your baby?"

The woman raised tired eyes from the newspaper. "*Si.*" She pointed to the buggy. "You have baby, too?"

"Yes." Rebecca nodded. "What is your baby's

name?" she asked, trying to sound friendly.

"Vincenza," replied the woman with a brief smile. "What your baby is called?"

"May I—may I hold your baby?" asked Rebecca, ignoring the question. She climbed the steps. The woman smiled, lay down the newspaper, and handed the fretful baby over. The baby screwed up her red face and yelled, then started sucking her fist. Rebecca opened the other little hand and looked at it closely. The nails had been neatly trimmed. She turned back the blanket to check a little foot as well. Yes, this was definitely the real Nora!

She looked down at the paper lying on the step. **Kidnapper Strikes Again** blared the headline. **Infant Girl Snatched Outside East-Side Pharmacy.**

"You like babies?" the woman was asking. "My girl Francesca, she like babies, too."

Rebecca stared wide-eyed, astonished at the way this woman could sit reading the newspaper as if she were innocent of the very crime emblazoned on the front page. What if *Vincenza* didn't really belong to the Martuscellis, even as Nora didn't? *I should jump down the steps and run with* both *babies,* thought Rebecca. How could she leave either one with a family of kidnappers?

The woman had picked up the paper again. "You know this word?" she asked, pointing at the front page. "I try to learn English. Is hard."

Rebecca looked at the fine print under the woman's finger. *"Attired,"* she read aloud. "It means what people wear."

Mrs. Martuscelli haltingly began reading. "'One-year-old Mabel Cameron was snatched'— snatched? That is meaning 'took'?"

"Taken," said Rebecca. "Kidnapped."

"Poor baby," said the woman, shaking her head. "Is bad thing."

As if she'd had nothing to do with it!

Mrs. Martuscelli continued reading, but Rebecca was not listening. She was tense, measuring the distance down the stoop, along the street, and around the corner. Her arms clutched Nora. *Go!* she told herself. *Just go!*

"*Snatched* from her buggy," the woman read aloud. "*Attired* in a white woolen coat and—"

Rebecca, planning the rescue, barely heard her voice. But the peal of a whistle broke into her desperate thoughts, and she looked up to see the welcome sight of a policeman—the very same freckle-faced policeman who had spoken to the girls in the park—hurrying along the street. He was chasing after three boys, who were running with a dog. *Francesca's puppy—and Luigi's gang!* This time Victor was not among them. With relief Rebecca realized she would not have to escape with both babies after all. She would just need to run to the officer's side and hand him the baby, and then Nora would be safe.

The policeman stopped the boys and shook his finger at them. Rebecca could tell he was ordering them to put a leash on that dog. The boys bowed their heads, as if ashamed. Luigi obediently picked up the puppy and carried him.

"Officer?" Rebecca called to him. "Officer!"

The woman looked up at her, alarmed. "What you are saying?"

The policeman walked over to the steps. "Those scalawags botherin' you, too, little lady?" the officer asked.

"No," said Rebecca. "They haven't been bothering me. But, well, it's another problem."

"There is *no problem!*" shouted a voice, and there was Francesca, emerging from the door of the tenement onto the stoop. She stood there, shaking her head at Rebecca. "Why you are here with my mama?" she demanded.

"I want Nora back."

"You got her, right there!" Francesca indicated the placid baby in the buggy at the bottom of the stoop.

"Calm down, lassies," said the police officer. "Let's hear what's wrong."

"Is nothing wrong here," said the woman, frowning. She reached for Nora. "I take my baby inside now," she said.

Rebecca shielded Nora and turned toward the policeman. "There *is* something wrong. There has been another kidnapping!" Rebecca raised her voice. "Not just the one in the paper.

A *different* sort of kidnapping. This baby—"

Francesca drowned out the accusation:
"Nothing is wrong! *Nothing at all!*"

"Lassies, lassies!" The policeman raised his
hands. "Both of you! Simmer down so I can
make sense of what you're saying."

"You're a liar!" Rebecca glared at the Italian
girl. "A liar and a —" she broke off with a gasp
at the sight of a man walking purposefully up
the sidewalk.

"Mr. Brodsky!" she cried. He had come just
in time to save his daughter!

"Why, hello, Rebecca," he called, looking
as surprised to see her as she was to see him.
"So, you're out on a walk with Nora?" He bent
down to smile at the baby in the buggy. Rebecca
watched him incredulously. *Why doesn't he notice
it isn't Nora lying there at all?* She looked down at
the baby in her arms. *Why doesn't he see that* this
is Nora?

"Goodness," he continued, "you're a long
way from home. Mrs. Brodsky said you had
gone to the park."

"Um—we did go to the park, but—" Before Rebecca could explain, he swung up the steps and onto the stoop.

"Good evening, Mrs. Martuscelli," he greeted the woman over the sounds of the baby, who had begun to wail in Rebecca's grasp. "I hope you're doing well, and your little one, too."

"You *know* Mrs. Martuscelli?" Rebecca squeaked out.

Mrs. Martuscelli plucked the crying baby out of Rebecca's arms.

The policeman still stood at the bottom of the steps, looking baffled. "So, is there a problem here? Officer Kelly, at your service."

"Problem?" Mr. Brodsky raised his eyebrows. "There's no problem—except how to get the last of our belongings to our new place." He smiled at Rebecca. "Good thing you've brought that buggy."

The policeman nodded and turned to Mrs. Martuscelli. "Is your boy toeing the line now, ma'am? Or still giving you heartache?"

The black-haired woman laughed, but her

eyes were anxious. "Ah, no, Officer Kelly. My Luigi, he a good boy! Sometimes he run a little wild, but—"

"My brother, he is doing nothing wrong!" Francesca interrupted, pushing forward. "He has good heart, not bad!" Her eyes sought Rebecca's, the expression pleading.

Rebecca's thoughts were whirling. Mr. Brodsky had lived here. He knew Mrs. Martuscelli!

Then Rebecca saw Luigi, the puppy in his arms, lurking behind a broken cart tipped over at the side of the curb. His friends had run off, and he was alone.

Rebecca blinked. She ran her mind over the facts. Someone was kidnapping babies in New York City. And someone had switched Nora and Vincenza. Francesca was the only one who could have made the switch—yet she was denying that it had happened at all. What on earth was going on here?

From the buggy came a little chuckle, and Mr. Brodsky stepped down to bend over the baby. "Hello, sweet Nora." Then he lifted the baby out and handed her to Rebecca. "I'll walk home with you," he said. "Let me just get the last box from our apartment."

Rebecca nodded wordlessly, looking at the baby in her arms, as Mr. Brodsky headed into the building.

Mrs. Martuscelli tucked the fussy baby into the crook of her arm in a practiced gesture, stroking the dark hair. "I am sorry about my boy, Luigi," she said to the officer. "He will keep the dog on the rope, you will see." The baby let out a louder squeal and kicked her legs. "I go in now. I need to feed this hungry girl."

"She's a handful, is she?" asked the policeman, smiling.

Mrs. Martuscelli nodded. "All my babies get the colic," she said, and she dipped her head to kiss the baby's cheek. "But they grow out of it." There was a glow in the woman's eyes as she gazed at the baby.

Rebecca tightened her grip on the baby in her own arms. *Whose baby was this?*

Mrs. Martuscelli lifted the baby and raised

one little hand to make her wave. "Say bye-bye, Vinnie, my heart."

The policeman laughed and waved good-bye.

Then Mrs. Martuscelli called down to Luigi. "And you! No more trouble—or it's off to Uncle Marco you go!" Mrs. Martuscelli kissed the baby again and went into the building.

Rebecca gazed at the scene, transfixed, as if she were watching a movie.

"So, missy." The policeman had turned to Rebecca. "Is everything all right then?"

She took a breath. Francesca jumped down the steps and stood next to her brother at the curb. Both of them looked at Rebecca, their faces anxious. The baby in Rebecca's arms regarded her with wide, calm eyes.

Nora—or Vincenza?

I think something very strange happened with the babies, Rose had said. And now Rebecca knew it was true. She exhaled slowly. Everyone waited. Francesca seemed to be holding her breath. "I guess . . . nothing is really wrong after all," said Rebecca.

He turned with a shrug. "If you say so. But if you need me, I'll be patrolling the park." He started walking down the street, then pivoted and pointed at Luigi. "You! No more trouble, you hear me, son?"

"Yes sir," said the boy, his face flaming. "I mean, no sir."

"Leave the laundry on the clotheslines!"

"Yes sir!"

The policeman walked away, swinging his nightstick. Luigi and Francesca watched him as he strolled slowly around the corner. When he was gone, the brother and sister edged toward the door of their tenement building.

"Hold on." Rebecca narrowed her eyes. "I want the truth about the babies."

"Nothing happened," began Francesca, and Luigi shook his head vehemently.

Rebecca laid the baby she was holding in the buggy and then turned to face them both. "I *know* you switched the babies," she began. "What I didn't realize was how many times you switched them."

"What?" demanded Francesca hotly, but she was looking sheepish.

"You crazy," said Luigi. His voice was tight.

"You know I'm not," Rebecca said steadily. She looked down at the baby, who gazed up at them from the buggy, chewing on her tin rattle. "This baby is not the same baby I took on the walk that day. Before I ever met the Brodskys, you must have switched the babies. And then in the park, *you switched them back again.*"

13
A CONFESSION

Francesca groaned and sank onto the step. Luigi gave Rebecca a wry smile. "Okay, you win," he said. "You very smart girl."

Rebecca sat down next to Francesca. "Tell me the truth."

"The truth?" said Francesca. "The truth is, my brother is not bad boy. Not in his heart." In a low, rapid voice, Francesca explained that Luigi and his pals often got into mischief.

Victor, Rebecca thought, nodding. Victor was in that group. That *gang*.

Twice Luigi had been brought home by the policeman, Francesca revealed—once for throwing a ball that broke a shop window and once for stealing apples from a cart at the market.

"Our parents were in a fury! They say he go

back to Italy to live with our uncle next time he is making trouble!"

Luigi grimaced. "Uncle Marco, he is very hard man. I do not like. I want to stay here with my own family." So he did shape up—until last Sunday morning, when he couldn't resist playing a trick on Francesca.

Luigi and Francesca took turns telling the story now. As if eager to unburden themselves, they talked over each other to be sure Rebecca understood all the details. It wasn't a very complicated story, really, Rebecca realized—but, oh, how many complications it had caused!

Early Sunday morning, the Brodskys had asked Francesca to look after Nora while they moved their belongings to their new apartment. "In your neighborhood, Rebecca," Francesca clarified.

"In our building!" said Rebecca.

Francesca continued. Mrs. Brodsky was having terrible problems with her eyes, and she needed to stay in a darkened room much of the time. Her poor eyesight must have been why

Mrs. Brodsky hadn't noticed that her baby's gown was soiled that morning. Francesca had carried Nora into the Martuscellis' apartment to change her.

"I'll just find you one of Vincenza's clean little gowns," Francesca had crooned to Nora, placing her on the bed. She dressed the Brodskys' baby in one of her own little sister's clean gowns.

"I make so many gowns for our baby Vincenza," Francesca told Rebecca. "So I can give one away to little Nora. And I sew the little golden corno."

"So that's why both babies were wearing identical gowns with the corno sewed into them!" exclaimed Rebecca. "You made them both!"

"*Sì*. Yes. For luck," said Francesca, nodding.

Luigi laughed. "Look, I have the corno, too." He turned up the hem of his ragged shirt, and there Rebecca saw the yellow threads stitched into a horn of blessing.

Francesca continued her account. Mr. Brodsky's friends and cousins had bustled in and out on moving day, packing boxes and trunks. They lugged furniture out of the building and lifted it onto handcarts. Francesca's job was to keep the baby out of the way.

Nora was always a peaceful baby, so it was easy to look after her as well as her own sister, Vincenza. Often Francesca had watched both babies while Mrs. Brodsky rested her eyes and Francesca's mother was busy with chores.

The autumn air had been brisk on Sunday morning, so Francesca bundled up both babies before taking them out to the street. Nora lay in her buggy, and her own baby sister lay in the wicker laundry basket that served as her bed. Vincenza was more fretful than usual with colic, or maybe she was teething. But being outside seemed to cheer her up. While the babies napped, Francesca skipped rope.

"I am very good jumping rope," she said to Rebecca now. "You like?"

"Yes!" said Rebecca. "But finish the story!" She glanced up at the door to the apartment. Mr. Brodsky would be out in a few minutes, and they would need to head home.

"What happened next," said Luigi, taking over, "was that our mama, she is calling out the window. She is saying Francesca must take care of our little brothers, too."

"Is hard." Francesca turned to Rebecca, shaking her head. "With *six* little brothers!" Counting on her fingers, she named each one: Carlo, Emilio, Dante, Armando, Federico, and Marco. "He is named for Uncle Marco, back in Italy."

On that Sunday morning when her mother had called out the window to her, Francesca had heaved a great sigh. She'd called for Luigi to look after the two babies while she ran inside to collect her brothers. Francesca had wished she could have just *one* day without taking care of any little children at all.

While she was indoors, Luigi had had an idea. "I decide to play trick on my sister," he told Rebecca with a flash of a grin. "I want to see how long before she notice."

And so he'd switched the Brodskys' sleeping

baby with his sister, tucking Nora into the basket, and tucking Vincenza—careful not to wake her because she was always so fussy—into Nora's buggy. He laid each baby on her belly, with her face turned to the side, and drew the covers up carefully. Then he wandered down the street with his puppy.

"Ha!" Luigi told Rebecca. "I am thinking I am very funny guy. I am thinking Francesca will get big surprise."

Francesca took over the story again. She had brought her little brothers outside to play ball while she watched the babies. Luigi had gone walking with the puppy. Before he returned, a man and woman came down the street and up to the stoop. Francesca had seen them earlier that day at the Brodskys', moving furniture.

"Hello," she said politely.

"Oh, hello," the man said. "I'm Frankel Brodsky, and this is my wife, Miriam. You must be Francesca. We've been sent to collect little Nora—and to give you this." Frankel Brodsky pressed a shiny nickel into Francesca's hand.

"Grazie!" she exclaimed at the unexpected gift. "Thank you!"

"Thank you for looking after her," said Miriam Brodsky. "Morris and Naomi wanted us to tell you they hope you will visit them soon in their new home." She took hold of the buggy and turned to go.

"Good-bye, little Nora." Francesca waved to the blanket-covered baby.

The cousins set off. Francesca went back to the ball game, when suddenly Luigi appeared with the puppy. He scanned the street, then grabbed her arm. *"La nostra sorellina!* Our little sister!" he rasped. They always spoke Italian together when they were alone. "Where is she?"

Francesca shook him off. "What do you mean, where is our sister?" She pointed at the basket. "Right there!"

"No! Where's the *buggy*?"

"Oh, some cousins came and took Nora to her new home. And they gave me a nickel!"

Luigi's voice was strained. "So ... did you like my trick? Wasn't it funny?"

"What are you talking about? What trick?"

"Oh, no," moaned Luigi, peering into the basket. The Brodskys' baby had rolled onto her back and was gazing up at him. "Vincenza is gone! The Brodskys have our Vinnie!"

"*What?*"

"Shh!" said Luigi.

Francesca looked into the buggy and gasped. "Luigi—what have you done?"

"Don't let the little fellas hear you," he begged. "They'll tell Mama! I'll get in so much trouble!"

"Oh, Luigi, *how could you?* You and your stupid pranks! We have to get the babies switched back right away! Before the Brodskys call the police!"

"How was I to know those cousins would come? Oh, Fran, I didn't mean any harm!"

"Look, we've got to do this fast," Francesca said. "We have to find out where the Brodskys have moved, and go there, and get back our baby sister ... "

❧

A Confession

"I see now," said Rebecca when Francesca and Luigi fell silent. "On Sunday morning my family was eating breakfast, and we could hear noises out in the hall. People were moving in, Mama said. We went over to meet them, and it was all a little crazy."

She remembered so clearly all the cousins and friends, and the howling baby, and Mama and Mrs. Henks both offering to help with Nora ... Rebecca blinked. There was something else she should remember. Something about Mama? Something about Nora? Something about Mrs. Henks?

"Mrs. Brodsky is asking you to look after baby?" Francesca asked.

"Well, my mama offered to take her," Rebecca recalled. "The baby was fussing so much, and Mr. Brodsky was leaving for work, and Mrs. Brodsky needed to lie down and rest her eyes. Everything was *busy*. I guess that's why no one recognized that the baby wasn't Nora. She was all bundled up. She was red in the face from crying.

"Mrs. Brodsky wasn't holding her, and Mr. Brodsky didn't hold her either because he was leaving. And the cousins didn't know her well enough to notice. I'm sure Nora's parents would have noticed once things settled down, but by then—"

"By then we make switch!" said Luigi triumphantly. "Was not long time the babies are with wrong families. Only until you come to the park."

Rebecca nodded. She saw now how it all had happened. Mama had taken the baby— the baby introduced to them as Nora—to their own apartment and away from the parents who would have known the difference.

Luigi said, "I ask my mama for Brodskys' new address, and then I run all the way to your street. I try to think how to grab my sister without anyone seeing!" He had seen Rebecca with the familiar buggy, strolling around the corner. He approached cautiously and peered in. Yes, there was his fretful sister. He had wished he could just lift her out of that buggy and run, but instead he'd smiled at the girl and said, "She is nice baby, no?"

Despite all the heartache and worry of the past few days, Rebecca felt a little sympathy for Luigi. "You must have been awfully scared," she said. "I'm just glad the babies are back with their real families."

"They always with real families," Francesca emphasized. "Except for maybe two hours. After we meet in park, you take real Nora home to her parents."

"The babies, they are never knowing they are switched," said Luigi. "And the parents are not noticing. So nobody is knowing—except *you*, Rebecca." He gave her an admiring glance. But under her steady gaze, his smile faded. "I hope policeman not send me to jail. Or my parents not send me to Uncle Marco!"

Rebecca frowned. Was all his concern just for himself? Didn't he care about the babies?

She reminded herself that Luigi had desperately tried to return the babies to their true families—and had succeeded in exchanging quiet Nora for his own colicky sister. A sudden realization washed over her. "So this means neither baby is sick!"

Francesca raised her dark eyebrows. "Our Vinnie is always healthy—just very loud." She smiled at Rebecca. "Don't forget. She has corno for a blessing!"

Rebecca smiled back. The babies were where they were supposed to be, and the Martuscellis weren't kidnappers. She felt as if a heavy stone had rolled off her conscience.

A chill wind sent dry leaves whirling down the street. Rebecca bent over Nora's buggy, where the baby had kicked off her blanket. Rebecca straightened the long gown, smiling at the yellow corno on the hem. The yellow was the same bright color as the little knit sweater and trousers that Mrs. Henks had thrown away—a sweater that would come in handy right now. Rebecca found it under the pillow and pulled it over little Nora's gown. How wasteful of Mrs. Henks to have thrown this pretty sweater out! Wouldn't a mother know another mother to pass garments on to when her children had outgrown them?

Mr. Brodsky came out of the tenement building carrying his last packing box as well as a ladies' dressmaking form. He placed the metal form carefully across the buggy, smiling down at Nora, who was tucked inside. "My wife said to leave the dressmaker's dummy behind," he told Rebecca, "but I must believe she'll get her sight back and work again." His voice was optimistic.

"I hope she will," Rebecca said, leaning over the metal frame to button the yellow sweater snugly around Nora. The baby gurgled at her—a contented, perfectly healthy little girl, her sweet face framed by her simple white bonnet. She was the right baby after all, even in another child's discarded clothing.

Another child. Again, a thought struggled to form, and Rebecca stood staring at the baby with a prick of unease. Mrs. Martuscelli's halting voice reading about baby clothes echoed in Rebecca's head. Rebecca had not been listening closely, but the woman had said something …

Rebecca wheeled around and darted past Mr. Brodsky, up the steps to the stoop. She snatched up the newspaper Mrs. Martuscelli had left on the chair. Her heart pounding, Rebecca scanned the article that Mrs. Martuscelli had struggled to read aloud.

Kidnapper Strikes Again

Infant Girl Snatched Outside Pharmacy

Yesterday afternoon young Mabel Cameron was snatched from her buggy outside Morton's Pharmacy while her grandmother shopped inside. The infant girl was attired in a white woolen coat and a bonnet of white lace embroidered with bluebells.

Rebecca dropped the newspaper. "Excuse me, Mr. Brodsky?" Her voice sounded strange to her—high-pitched and tight. "Have you lost Nora's other bonnet?"

He looked puzzled. "Other bonnet? She has only one." He pointed to his daughter in the buggy. "The one she's wearing. Why do you ask?"

Only one bonnet. And yet a bonnet had been lying on the sidewalk outside Rebecca's building last night. A white lace bonnet embroidered with blue flowers.

And the nice yellow knit garments had lain in the trash.

And both times the same person had been there.

"Something is wrong?" asked Francesca.

Leaving the others staring after her, Rebecca jumped down the steps and ran toward the park as fast as she could. "Police!" she shouted. "Police!"

14
BRAVE AND BOLD AS A QUEEN

Rebecca's woolen cape flew out like a sail as she raced toward the park. As she ran, she tried to put her tumbling thoughts into coherent order.

Mrs. Henks had told the Brodskys she lived right in their neighborhood, but later she told Rebecca she lived by the park. Mrs. Henks had been leaning over Nora's buggy outside the pharmacy where Rebecca had gone to buy the salve. Mrs. Henks had thrown away a bundle of perfectly good baby clothes. Mrs. Henks and the man in the bowler hat had passed by in the street just before Rebecca found the bonnet on the ground—and the paper today reported another baby had been kidnapped, a baby wearing a bonnet just like the one on the street . . .

Rebecca was panting now as she raced through the park entrance. She stopped and scanned the paths.

Clusters of people were hurrying homeward, some carrying shopping baskets. A tired mother holding two young children by the hands tugged them past the swings. An old man who had been selling hot chestnuts near the pond trundled his cart across the grass. Was Mrs. Henks still here in the park?

Where was Officer Kelly?

Rebecca passed a man sitting on a bench, an open newspaper held up in front of him. As she ran by, the man dropped the paper and stood up. "Rebecca," he said, "May I have a word with you, please?"

It was the man in the bowler hat! Startled, Rebecca stopped.

"I think you are an observant girl," he continued in a low, confidential voice. "I'd like to talk with you."

Rebecca's relief made her giddy. "Are you— are you an undercover policeman? I've seen you with Mrs. Henks! So you suspect her, too?"

"Yes," he said in a hushed voice. "Could you please come with me?"

She saw a flash of uniform over by the pond. "Officer Kelly!" she called, hoping it was him. Now she could tell both policemen what she suspected. "Over here—"

Her cry was cut off abruptly when a hand in a black glove slapped over her mouth. "Quiet," growled a soft voice in her ear. Rebecca struggled in the iron grip of the man in the bowler hat. And suddenly Mrs. Henks was there, too, pressing against Rebecca's other side. Together Mrs. Henks and the man started to march her toward the gate.

He's not *a policeman,* realized Rebecca in panic. *They're in this together!*

The man removed his hand from her mouth but did not release her arm. "Stay quiet," he warned, "or you'll be very, very sorry."

"Be meek and still as a mouse," Mrs. Henks hissed. She linked her arm tightly through Rebecca's.

"We can't have little girls running around in distress, now, can we?" The man's voice was calm but tense. "We can't have them summoning the police."

Rebecca opened her mouth to shout for help—even if Officer Kelly had not heard her call, surely one of the people strolling through the park would come to her aid. But Mrs. Henks and the man steered Rebecca across the grass, away from the pond, and toward the park gate. Fear made her mouth dry.

"You're the kidnappers!" she whispered. "You've been following me!" She struggled to free herself.

"Let's just say we've been keeping an eye on you since you started snooping in trash cans," said Mrs. Henks. Gone was the warm, friendly voice. "Now, not another sound."

Mama's voice echoed in Rebecca's head. *A lady doesn't make a display of herself.* Rebecca tightened her trembling lips so that she wouldn't start screaming.

Then, dizzily, Rebecca remembered Queen

Esther, who had not been quiet or meek. She had been strong and courageous. *A lady is bold when she needs to be.* Bubbie's voice sounded in Rebecca's head, almost as if her grandmother were right there with her.

Rebecca kicked fiercely. "Kidnappers!" she shouted. She bit fiercely at the gloved hand that came up to clamp over her mouth again. *"Help!"* she cried, jabbing her elbows, kicking and yelling like a wild creature. Were they counting on her being too afraid to make a scene? She would show them differently!

Two women raced over from the swings, calling out, "What is it? What's wrong?" The man with the chestnuts abandoned his cart and sprinted toward her. And from the corner of her eye, she saw Luigi and Francesca coming through the park gate.

"Help!" screamed Rebecca.

As people converged on them, Rebecca's attackers dropped her arms and bolted. Luigi reached out and caught Rebecca as she stumbled. She saw a flash of navy blue—Officer Kelly!

"Calm down, little lady," he said, raking Luigi with his gaze. "Leave her be, you scalawag!"

Luigi dropped Rebecca's arm, looking very frightened. "I wasn't—"

"He was helping me," said Rebecca urgently. "It's Mrs. Henks you need to catch—and that man." She scanned the street, pointing. "Look, there they go now!" Mrs. Henks and the man in the bowler hat were melting away through the park gate. "They are the kidnappers, I'm sure of it!"

Officer Kelly set off running down the sidewalk. Luigi tore after him, and Francesca followed. Rebecca crossed the street, trying to circle around and head the pair off at the corner.

"Rebecca?" someone shouted. "Rebecca, what are you doing?" Mr. Brodsky was coming toward her, pushing the buggy awkwardly over the bumpy sidewalk, trying to keep the dressmaker's frame from falling off. His face was a mask of astonishment as Mrs. Henks and the man careened toward him, chased by Officer Kelly, Luigi, and Francesca.

Rebecca leaped forward and shoved the dressmaker's dummy off the buggy—and straight into their path.

It crashed to the pavement, and Mrs. Henks tripped over it, tumbling to her knees. The man knocked into her and fell heavily at her side. In a flash the officer was upon him, nightstick raised in one hand, the other pulling a pair of handcuffs from his coat pocket. Luigi held tightly to Mrs. Henks, who knelt silently now, head bowed.

"What in tarnation?" exclaimed Mr. Brodsky.

From the buggy, Nora's frightened wail pierced the air. It was the first time, Rebecca thought giddily, that she had ever heard the real Nora cry. Mr. Brodsky peered down at the baby anxiously.

Rebecca took a deep breath. Adrenaline— and elation—coursed through her veins. She had done it. She had made a great big unladylike scene—and it had worked!

Officer Kelly took over. "I'll need statements from all of you," he said, "and then I'll get these two down to the station."

Rebecca described how her suspicions were raised when she learned that the baby bonnet she had found in the street matched the bonnet worn by the kidnapped baby girl. She had found the bonnet just after Mrs. Henks and the man in the bowler hat passed by in the middle of the night. Maybe the kidnapped baby had been in that basket they were carrying! And just now, Mrs. Henks and this man had tried to stop Rebecca when she was looking for a police officer to tell.

The man in handcuffs snarled to Mrs. Henks. "Soon as I saw her snooping in the trash can that day, I knew she was trouble. I told you."

"It was *you* who told me to toss the clothes," Mrs. Henks snapped back. "All this was your idea in the first place!"

"Save it for the trial," said Officer Kelly. He looked at the others. "You're free to go. Thank you for your help. Lad, help me convey these two to the station."

"My pleasure, sir," Luigi said grandly.

Mr. Brodsky scooped Nora out of the buggy. The baby screwed up her face and let out another yell. "Rebecca," he said, "what in the world is going on?"

She gave her neighbor a shaky grin. "Nora sounds ready for her supper. I'll tell you all about it on the way home!"

15

SO MUCH TO CELEBRATE

Rebecca told Mr. Brodsky everything she knew about the kidnappers, but she kept to herself the story of how two look-alike babies had been switched. When they reached home, they handed Nora to Mrs. Brodsky, and together they climbed the stairs to Rebecca's apartment.

"That was a very long walk," Papa greeted her. "Why, good evening, Mr. Brodsky." He looked surprised to see their neighbor behind her.

Mama came in from the kitchen, hands on her hips. "You're just in time for dinner—" She broke off at the sight of Mr. Brodsky.

"Your daughter has had quite a shock," said Mr. Brodsky. "But she became a hero today!"

Rebecca's family gathered in the parlor as

Mr. Brodsky and Rebecca related what had taken place in the park. Papa sat down hard in his armchair, looking stunned. Mama said that she felt faint at the thought of the danger Rebecca had been in. The twins and Benny stared at their sister in astonishment, but Victor grinned and gave her a thumbs-up. Rebecca glowed from his unexpected approval.

Then Papa and Mama thanked Mr. Brodsky, and he went back to his own family.

Mama fussed over Rebecca at dinner, and bundled her into bed afterward with a hot water bottle. "After such a dangerous adventure, you need to rest," she said.

Sophie and Sadie sat on Rebecca's bed, pelting her with questions until Papa drew them out of the room. "Leave your sister to sleep," he said. Then he laid one hand on Rebecca's head. "You were very brave this afternoon."

"Foolhardy!" Mama cried, stroking Rebecca's cheek. "You were nearly kidnapped yourself!"

"I'm sorry," Rebecca murmured. She closed her eyes, remembering the slap of the man's gloved hand across her mouth. She shivered, and Mama drew up the quilt.

"Sleep," she said. "I'm sure the police will find the stolen baby girl now, thanks to you!"

But as Rebecca lay snugly in bed, sleep did not come. *I must tell them*, she thought hazily, *I must tell them about Nora*.

Images of Francesca and Luigi kept playing behind her eyes like a movie. Oh, what those two with their pranks and their lies had put her through! But it had all been a mistake, and nobody had been hurt, and nothing bad had happened. In fact, Rebecca admired how Luigi and Francesca, though scared, had tried their hardest to fix things. Perhaps now they could all be friends. Finally she drifted off to sleep.

But in the night she awakened, certain she had heard the scrape of the bolt on the front door. Was Victor sneaking out again? Or returning after . . . after doing *what*? Now that she wasn't worrying about Luigi, though, or about kidnappers, she fell back to sleep, too tired to investigate.

A Bundle of Trouble

✤

In the morning, Benny woke the family early. "Come on, everybody! I need to show you something before we go to school!" He urged them to get dressed and follow him, insisting there was no time for breakfast first. "We need to go upstairs," he said mysteriously.

"What are you up to?" Mama asked sleepily.

"And where's Victor?" Rebecca asked.

Mama and Papa exchanged a perplexed look. "Victor must be having breakfast with Bubbie and Grandpa," Mama said. "But on a school day?"

The twins heaved a sigh. "We love Bubbie's pancakes! Why didn't she invite us?" asked Sadie.

Rebecca and her family followed Benny up the stairs. "I'll run ahead and get Bubbie and Grandpa," he said. "Wait here!"

Though the morning had dawned bright outside the Rubins' windows, very little sunlight reached the stairwell. The family waited on the landing while Benny knocked on the door of their grandparents' apartment.

Bubbie and Grandpa opened the door, tying the sashes on their dressing gowns. "My goodness!" exclaimed Bubbie when she saw everyone on the stairs. "What is this, a party?"

Peering past them, Rebecca saw no sign of Victor in their kitchen.

"Come on," laughed Benny as he started up the stairs.

Rebecca followed the others, bemused. It was nice to see Benny back to being his cheerful self. But where was Victor?

They climbed the stairs to the top of the building. And as Benny tugged open the heavy door leading onto the roof, Rebecca suddenly realized what Victor had been doing late at night.

"*Ta-da!*" cried Benny.

There was Victor, grinning at them all. "Good morning, and welcome to our sukkah!"

Proudly he led them to a three-sided wooden frame with a roof of leafy branches. The roof was partly open so that people inside could see the sky. The autumn sun shone through the leaves, dappling the table Victor had made from two sawhorses and some planks of wood. He had brought up one of Mama's tablecloths to cover the table and had arranged apples, dried flowers and corn, and a pumpkin as a center-piece. Bunches of grapes, tied with string, hung in the doorway.

"I built it myself," Victor said. "After school and"—he yawned widely—"late at night."

Victor ushered them all inside the sukkah with great fanfare and offered Bubbie the single chair. "So that's why you needed my desk chair," said Grandpa, eyes twinkling.

Benny seated the others on upturned wooden crates. "I helped," he said proudly. "I went to the neighbors and asked if they had crates we could borrow. Mrs. Brodsky gave me *three*, because I helped her finish unpacking."

"Told you I wasn't the kidnapper," Victor whispered in Rebecca's ear. She sensed that her brother was relieved to be back in the good graces of the family.

"Both of you boys did a wonderful job," Mama said, "We'll eat our meals here all week. We have a lot to be thankful for." She put an arm around Rebecca and hugged her tightly.

⚜

That night the Brodskys joined Rebecca's family on the rooftop. They spilled out of the sukkah onto packing boxes and quilts. Mrs. Brodsky sat with Nora on her lap, wrapped in a shawl. Candles burning in the sukkah lit the rooftop with a warm glow.

Below them, Rebecca could see clotheslines strung between the buildings. She could hear children playing in the street. The lights of their neighborhood shone from hundreds of windows.

As Mama and Bubbie bustled about, laying out the meal, Mr. Brodsky handed Papa the evening newspaper. "Have you seen your own Rebecca in the paper?" he asked.

Papa took the newspaper and opened it.

Sadie leaned close to see. "Rebecca's a hero!"

"And the whole city knows it," Sophie added, as Rebecca flushed.

"Please read to us," urged Mrs. Brodsky.

Papa smiled. "With pleasure."

Kidnappers Caught By 11-Year-Old Girl

Two kidnappers were brought to justice yesterday by eleven-year-old Rebecca Rubin, whose tip to the police after a confrontation in Tompkins Square Park led to the arrest. After extensive interrogation, the couple confessed to a string of similar kidnappings in Philadelphia three years ago and to two more recently in Boston.

Papa peered over the top of the newspaper. "Mrs. Henks confessed everything to the police," he said. "It seems she and her husband targeted babies who were left waiting outside while their mothers ran errands. She would send her husband inside the shop to create a diversion while she snatched the child. They then disguised the babies by changing their hair and clothing. There's a quote here from Mrs. Henks," said Papa as he continued to scan the article. "She said to the police, 'We never hurt anybody. We always returned the babies. How is that so terrible?'" Papa shook his head.

"It chills my bones to think that woman came to our door and offered to look after Nora!" Mrs. Brodsky cried.

"How lucky we are that the Rubins took her home that day," said Mr. Brodsky, putting his arm around his wife's shoulders. "Or we might have been the next family trying to raise a ransom."

"What about the kidnapped baby girl?" Rebecca asked urgently. "Mabel Cameron?"

"Oh, yes," Papa said, scanning the article. "She is safely home with her parents."

He folded the paper, smiling proudly at Rebecca. Relieved, she turned to help Mama cut the loaves of bread as Bubbie sent Sadie downstairs to bring up more butter.

When Sadie returned, Luigi and Francesca

were with her. "I found them outside our door," Sadie said.

"We come to visit," Francesca said shyly, looking at the candlelit sukkah with wide, dark eyes. She took Rebecca's arm and led her away from the others. Her voice was low and confidential. "When my parents see us come home with policeman last night, they very angry at first. They say Luigi must go to Uncle Marco. But then the policeman say we both help to catch the kidnappers. So they very happy."

"I'm glad," said Rebecca. "Now please come meet my family." She took Francesca's hand and started toward the sukkah, but Francesca pulled back, a look of panic in her eyes.

"Oh, I cannot. Look—Brodskys are here!"

"Don't worry," whispered Rebecca. "We won't tell them about the babies being switched. After all, there was no harm done."

Francesca beamed at her.

No, Rebecca decided, she would never tell the Brodskys, but she would tell her family the whole story, and she would tell Rose, too. No one would say she was dramatizing this time!

"Who are your friends, Beckie?" Mama called to her.

Rebecca introduced Francesca and Luigi to the rest of her family. Victor jumped up and clapped Luigi on the back. The Brodskys were delighted to see their old neighbors again.

"How nice that you have come to visit," said Mrs. Brodsky. "I'm hoping your mother will also visit once we are settled."

"It's good to meet you both," Mama said warmly. "Please share in our feast. It is the first night of Sukkos, and we have plenty."

"Thank you," replied Francesca softly, and Luigi nodded.

"So you are Luigi," Papa said. "We have heard a lot about you."

Uh-oh. Rebecca hoped he was not going to mention the pranks Luigi and Victor had played. She let out her breath when Papa shook Luigi's hand. "The newspaper says you dived right in to help the police," Papa said with approval.

"Yes, sir," said Luigi, bowing his head.

"Come tell us about it," Papa urged.

Luigi's eyes sparkled. "It is really Rebecca who is stopping the kidnappers. I just help catch them when they try to run away."

Inside the sukkah, the meal was ready. Mama had prepared all the Sukkos foods Rebecca loved: fresh fruits and vegetables, cabbage stuffed with meat, and oven-baked potatoes. Bubbie had baked loaves of fresh bread, and the Brodskys had contributed a honey cake.

Mama and Papa said the Sukkos blessings. Then everyone feasted and talked, pulling on coats and shawls when the evening air grew brisk. No one wanted to leave the circle of candlelight and good company to go back downstairs.

After a while, they grew silent, and Mr. Brodsky pulled out his fiddle. Rebecca lay back on a blanket with Francesca at her side. The haunting melody seemed to float over the rooftops of New York. Mrs. Brodsky hummed along, eyes closed, cuddling baby Nora.

Rebecca thought of other babies—Vincenza, home with the Martuscellis, and little Mabel Cameron, safe tonight with her family, somewhere in New York City under this same dark sky. She felt a great sense of peace. On this Sukkos, there was much to be thankful for.

"Beckie?" whispered Francesca. "You will come to the park again? You are walking there tomorrow, maybe?"

"Yes, let's go after school tomorrow," Rebecca replied, turning to smile at her new friend. "But this time, we'll leave the babies at home and bring our jump ropes instead!"

LOOKING BACK

A PEEK INTO THE PAST

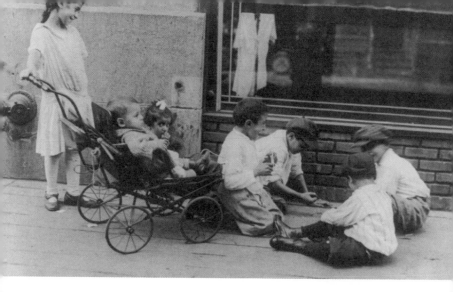

When Rebecca and Francesca chatted and
played as the babies in their charge napped,
they had lots of company. While mothers were
busy doing housework, their daughters became
baby-minders at a very young age. These "little
mothers" would feed, hold, or rock their baby
siblings to sleep. When they took their
younger siblings outside for fresh
air, they would chat with friends,
do needlework, jump rope, or
play hopscotch while keeping a
careful eye on the baby carriage.

A girl holds her sleeping baby sister.

Their brothers were not expected to help as much with child care, but many young boys sold newspapers or did other work to bring in extra money for their households. As boys got older, their sense of adventure lured them further from home and into friendships with boys from different backgrounds. Like

A newsboy sells papers on the street.

Victor and Luigi, they watched out for each other and sometimes performed pranks and gained reputations for mischief. They annoyed their neighbors by loosening the ropes on clotheslines, playing tag on roofs, or bouncing balls against doors and front stoops. Police patrolling the neighborhoods regularly chased these bands of boys from the streets and threatened them with arrest, but generally their mischief wasn't criminal. In fact, like Victor, many of these boys were good students and had a good upbringing.

Boys gambling in the streets

Most neighborhoods were safe places to play. Children played on the sidewalks and streets while their mothers kept an eye on them through windows that faced the street. Mothers and girls often left babies outside in carriages while they briefly entered a shop. But they learned to be more careful when reports of kidnappings appeared in the newspapers.

Though child kidnappings were rare, when they happened they received a lot of attention in the newspapers, and parents became very concerned, just as Rebecca's family did. Most child kidnappings were done by petty criminals who didn't want to harm a child but wanted to collect money for its return. In one case, a woman invited a fruit peddler into her apartment. As she was choosing bananas, the peddler snatched her four-year-old daughter and ran out. The door locked behind

Articles about kidnappings were front-page news.

him as it slammed shut, and the woman climbed through her open front window, shouting for help as she ran after the kidnapper. Neighbors joined the chase, and the kidnapper was quickly caught.

Often the family of a kidnapped child received a ransom letter demanding they leave a sum of money in a certain spot

The most famous infant kidnapping took place in 1932, when the son of famed aviator Charles Lindbergh was abducted.

and cautioning them not to notify police. In spite of the warning, some parents did tell the police, and the kidnappers were caught. Other parents took heed of the kidnappers' warnings but had little money, so sympathetic neighbors sometimes took up a collection to help ransom the child.

To keep family members safe from misfortune, some immigrants turned to traditional customs that they carried with them from the Old Country. One common practice in Italian families like the Martuscellis was wearing a charm called a *corno*, which means "horn" in English. The charms were given to children at birth to protect them from harm. In this story, the author has imagined that the corno was stitched onto the baby's clothing for good luck, since

A girl wears a corno charm around her neck.

a baby was too young to wear a charm!

Immigrant families also brought their traditional celebrations with them to America. In the fall, Jewish families celebrated a holiday to give thanks for the abundance of life. It was

A mother and daughter outside their family's sukkah in 2009

called Sukkos (SUHK-us) in Rebecca's time and is pronounced Sukkot (soo-COAT) today. As part of the celebration, families build small outdoor shelters like the temporary dwellings once built by the Israelites, with a roof loosely covered with leafy tree branches. Friends and family are invited to share meals in the shelter.

Building the temporary shelter serves to remind people that many of the things we wish for are only fleeting pleasures. What matters is that we live according to our values. This lesson is one that families like the Rubins hoped to teach their children.

GLOSSARY OF ITALIAN WORDS

corno *(KOR-no)*—horn; an Italian good-luck charm shaped like an animal's horn

grazie *(GRAHT-zee-eh)*—thank you

la nostra sorellina *(la NO-strah so-rel-EE-nah)*—our little sister

le mie principesse *(leh MEE-eh prin-chi-PEH-seh)*—my princesses

sì *(see)*—yes

ABOUT THE AUTHOR

 As a girl, Kathryn Reiss loved poking around in her grandmother's attic, finding books, photographs, and toys from past generations. She enjoyed hearing about her grandparents' childhood adventures and loved reading stories set in the early twentieth century. Although she grew up in Ohio—where she used to babysit for all the babies and children in her neighborhood—she spent one memorable summer in New York City when she was Rebecca's age, exploring the city with her brother and looking for mysteries. She started writing mysteries herself because nothing eerie or unusual ever seemed to happen in her own life!

Ms. Reiss's previous novels of suspense have won many awards. She lives with her husband and their five nearly grown children in northern California, where she teaches creative writing at Mills College.